I0689161

Beyond Lace

A Hard Men of the Rockies Novella

Mia London

Beyond Lace
by Mia London

This is a work of fiction. Names, characters, places and incidents either are the product of the author's imagination or are used factitiously, and any resemblance to actual persons, living or dead, business establishments, event or locales is entirely coincidental.

September 2016
ISBN # 978-0-9905274-6-6 Electronic
ISBN # 978-0-9905274-7-3 Print

Publisher: Mia London
PO Box 93852
Southlake, TX 76092

Cover illustrator: www.sweetnspicydesigns.com
Interior Design by: www.PolgarusStudio.com

The entire Hard Men of the Rockies
novella series:

Red Lace by Kym Roberts
Tango & Lace by Misty Dietz
Leather & Lace by Brynley Bush
Beyond Lace by Mia London
Blackmail & Lace by Tracy A. Ward

Titles by Mia London

Beyond Lace, A Hard Men of the Rockies Novella
Life To The Max
Perfect Seduction, Perfect Series #1
Perfect Surrender, Perfect Series #2
Wanton Angel **coming soon*

Special Thanks

Thank you Brynley, Kym, Misty, and Tracy! Collaborating with you awesome, smart, and funny women while making this Hard Men of the Rockies series was amazing!

LETTER TO MY READERS:

Hello my dear readers,

I am so excited you chose to read my book. When I was asked to join the *Chick Swaggers* for this series, I was excited and nervous. Excited to be part of the collaboration, but nervous about living up to any expectations. It turned out to be one of my best decisions.

The *chicks* told me about the premise of the series and that "Lace," in any form or fashion, needed to be part of the title and story.

Thinking about the story, it hit me. Lace wasn't a thing; it was a place. From there, the creative energy carried me. Lace is a town outside Fort Collins, Colorado. It is pronounced "lacy" after the family that settled it back in 1867. It is where Blake and Charlie grew up and went to school. Ironically, they didn't really know each other until college at CSU. And the fireworks between them were undeniable.

Enjoy this story and the series of cousins coming to Fort Collins to help their sweet, feisty grandmother.

If you are so inclined, we would all love a review; it tells us more about what you would like to read in the future.

I appreciate you, and thanks for being loyal to romance!

Mia

Prelude

Blake Strickland shoved his tablet and printouts into his computer bag and grabbed the last of the coffee before heading out the door.

His condo neighbor, a friendly old woman, strolled down the stairs with her chihuahua tethered by a leash.

"Good morning, Mrs. Parker."

"Oh, good morning, Blake. Off bright and early?"

"Yes, ma'am," he replied as he sidled passed.

"You work too much. You need to find yourself a nice woman and settle down."

He forced a smile her way.

He'd heard that sentiment before . . . from Mrs. Parker, from his mother, from his aunts. He couldn't make them understand *settling down* was not his thing. Not by any stretch of the imagination.

Blake stopped short when a two-inch scratch on the bumper of his European sports car caught his eye. *Shit!* He paid extra for this secluded parking spot. Well, he would have to deal with it later; there was nothing he could do about it now.

He pulled away from Park Ridge and merged south onto I-90, heading for downtown Chicago. The radio played some classic rock and roll, not that it mattered. His mind was already on business. That was his modus operandi—think about work before, during, and after work. Occasionally, he could be distracted by a basketball game, a poker night, a few hours with a woman, or writing code for an app. People called him a workaholic. He didn't care; his devotion to his career had led him to success.

Two years ago, he sold his first internet company for several million dollars. He was twenty-seven at the time. And Blake wasn't ashamed to admit he was working tirelessly on his next company. His goal—to grow it to the point where he could sell it for a handsome profit.

His thoughts were interrupted by a phone call. The screen on his dashboard read Jackson Whiteside, his cousin.

"Hi, Jack. How's it goin'?"

"Hey, Blake. I'm good, man. How's life in the concrete jungle?"

"More comfortable than sweating it out in the Middle East digging up old scrolls written by men in white beards, I'm sure."

Jack laughed. "At least I don't sit on my ass staring at a computer screen all day, every day. You hear about grandma?"

Blake wondered when he'd get the call from one of his cousins. His mom had called him the week prior to tell him that his grandmother, his father's mother, had suffered a heart attack. Medical reports showed she was fine, but needed time to recuperate.

"Yeah, I heard. How's she doing?"

"She'll bounce back. I just got to Fort Collins. Ty's been here for a while now."

"How's he feeling?" Blake couldn't imagine what the recovery was like from a gunshot wound.

"Real good. In fact, we just finished up reshingling her roof. Since I'm here, he'll be heading back to Noble Pass tomorrow. We decided we need to take turns staying with grandma. Give her some company and fix up the house. The exterior looks like shit, and who knows what needs tinkering on the inside. She can't do it by herself."

"Okay," Blake said, drawing out the word.

"So, man up. I'll be here through July, and Knox said he'd come after football camp in August. That means you're on deck in September."

Why the hell did he need to go to Fort Collins? "I thought Mya looked after her."

"I'm not discussing Mya." Jack's voice hardened.

"Touchy much?"

"Rosie's our blood, our responsibility."

"You're right."

"That's why I'm calling now. Give you time to plan, Mister Big Wig."

"Whatever."

All the cousins were successful in their own right. They were good men, and Blake's only regret about them was that they didn't live closer to each other. Since he didn't have any siblings, his cousins were like brothers to him.

"So can you make it?"

He exhaled. "Yeah, I'll make it." But it was the *last* place on God's green earth he wanted to be.

"And leave your monkey suits at home. You'll need *real* work clothes. The place needs some TLC."

"Shit."

Jack chuckled over the phone. He loved to antagonize him. "Hang in there, big man. I'll see you when you get here." The line disconnected.

Blake stared at the road ahead. *Well, that's just great.* Going back to Fort Collins, Colorado wasn't his idea of fun. He loved his grandmother, that wasn't the issue. He'd do anything for her. What he didn't want was to run into Charlotte Brookfield. Charlie.

It had been eight years since he saw her last. What a fucking fiasco.

He cranked the fan on the car's air conditioner.

There was a bright side. He'd heard Charlie moved back to Lace after graduation. Her entire family lived in Lace. Chances were good that he could get in and get out without so much as hearing her name. He nodded to no one. *Yup. Get in, get out.*

Chapter One

The summer flew by.

Blake spoke to Ty and Jack again. He and Knox had traded emails. And in the time it took to defrag a hard drive, September was here.

He felt a knot in his stomach all morning as he heaved some more t-shirts and toiletries into his duffle bag. Next, he fished out his climbing gear—gloves, slippers, and canteen—from the back of his closet. His flight to Denver would depart at noon. His friend, Damen, would drive him to O'Hare.

He zipped his bag and dropped it at the front door. He checked his laptop case—tablet, computer, charger, mouse, files, phone charger, pens, and highlighters.

He sucked in a deep breath. Why was he so jacked up? He shouldn't give one shit about going to Fort Collins. His grandma needed him, so there was no question—he would go. So why the hell did Charlie invade his thoughts now more than ever?

Over the past few years, she'd popped into his mind now

and again. Nothing serious. Flashbacks of holding her close after sex—her smell intoxicating. Random women would cross his path and remind him of Charlie—the way a svelte brunette sashayed her hips, a woman at the deli who ordered a turkey-cheese sandwich with sliced gherkins inside, or the sweet citrusy scent of a woman's fragrance. And when she occupied his dreams, he'd wake up hard with her on his mind.

Nothing really noteworthy. He was so fucking over her, it wasn't even funny.

A knock came from his door. Damen. *No turning back now.*

When he arrived at the car rental company at Denver International, he decided to upgrade to an SUV. He'd much rather tool around the mountains in an SUV than a practical sedan. Driving off the lot, he lowered the car window and let the fresh air in.

He inhaled the fresh mountain air and smiled. His first smile in a while.

Seeing the mountains in the distance got Blake's heart revving for rock climbing.

Climbing had been Blake's love since his diaper days. His dad would take him to spots near Lace, starting with small hills. As he grew, he and his dad would conquer bigger hills and boulders, working their way up to climbing the mountains. By his teen years, Blake would venture out on his own, and life was good.

Not much rock climbing in Illinois. He grimaced.

After an hour on the road, he pulled into the drive at Rosie's house. Jack hadn't lied. The place needed some repairs. Bushes were overgrown, window screens had tears, and flowerbeds were filled with weeds.

"Blake!" his grandma called from the front porch. "How are you? I've missed you."

Blake dropped his duffle bag and swung his arms around the five-one, little dynamo of a grandmother and lifted her off her feet.

"Hi, Grandma." He kissed her cheek. "How are you feeling? I've missed you, too."

She patted his cheek as he set her down.

"My, how handsome you are." Then, she flapped her hand at him. "Come. Get your things. Let's go inside. I want to hear everything."

Blake hid his smile. He had nothing to tell.

Blake followed his grandmother inside and set his bag down at the foot of the steps.

"Grandma," he started, "you look good. How are you feeling?"

"Dear, I'm feeling pretty good." She took a seat at the kitchen table, and he joined her. "Of course, I have medicine to take now until the day I die." She rolled her eyes. "And I need to make some minor changes to my routine."

"What kind of changes?" He frowned.

"Well, I need to cut out a lot of red meat and eat more fish. I have supplements that my doctor wants me to take, and I walk several times a week."

"Grandma, you were always pretty active." Plus, she was fun and feisty, always seeing the good in everyone.

She smiled. "Yes, but even I've slowed down the last few years."

He nodded.

"I also need to eat less salt and sugar. Not having salt isn't so bad, but you know how I love my desserts." She grinned.

"Yes, I do." Blake recalled times when she'd give him and his cousins popsicles during the summer. They'd eat them outside and Grandma always had at least one, too.

She reached forward and stroked the back of his hand. "You know sweetie, I don't mind the changes. Life has been good to me. If I can get a few more years, that's all I can ask. Your grandfather will have to wait." She chuckled at her own joke.

He smiled, thankful she had survived the heart attack and could sit there with him now, laughing and joking.

"So, you have turned into an exceptional businessman, Blake. I am so proud of you. How is your company?" Her eyes twinkled.

"It's good. The business is growing. I'd like to get it to the point where I can sell it like last time. We'll see." He lifted a shoulder.

"Is it okay for you to be away this long?"

"Sure. I brought my computer. I can work from here." He would never tell her how hard it was to leave.

"Terrific. I'll bet you're excited to see your old friends again. You don't have to be with me all the time, you know. I want you to make plans, go out, have some fun. Okay?"

"I will, Grandma."

Seeing friends from college. Yes, that would be a good thing. He was anxious to do some rock climbing, too. Those are the things he'd focus on because just being back in Colorado set his nerves on edge.

His skin prickled thinking about his old girlfriend and knowing how close in proximity they were now.

Charlie had been the love of his life. His one and only love. They'd met their senior year at Colorado State, and the chemistry had been instantaneous. That quickly grew to love. He'd envisioned a future with her. Then she'd cheated and brought everything to a screeching halt.

Get in, get out. Get in, get out.

Chapter Two

Charlie walked into Catwalk, a local bar, with her good friend, Lori. They have been best friends since the fourth grade and loved to blow off the stress of the day at the local haunts. The crowd seemed like the usual Fort Collins group for a Friday night.

Lori and Charlie scanned the room for any open tables, and Charlie's eyes landed on a man sipping a beer with his back to her. He had a familiar frame, but she couldn't place it. Was he someone who worked with one of her clients?

"I don't see a table. Do you?" Not waiting for a response, Lori suggested, "Let's go to the bar and wait for something to open up."

Charlie nodded, then focused her attention back to the stranger. He sat at the far end of the bar and slanted her direction when he called out to the bartender.

She stumbled for a second.

That looks like Blake. The thought popped into her head with a suddenness of a bottle rocket. She stared. Her heart pounded in her chest, on the verge of exploding.

Lori asked her something, but she couldn't even hear it. "Hey."

She glanced at her friend. "What?"

"What do you want to drink?"

"Um. A beer."

Her attention back on the man, she strained to get a clear view over the horde of people. It was very unlikely Blake. Her imagination was getting the best of her. She watched as he ordered another drink from Larry. Even his mannerisms seemed like Blake's.

She turned straight ahead. The blood thundered in her ears.

"Oh shit," she breathed.

"What is it?" Lori asked.

She faced her friend.

"You alright, sweetie?" Lori asked as she placed a hand on Charlie's arm. "Your face is sheet-white."

"Lori, the man at the other end of the bar, third stool." She motioned with her head. "Doesn't that look like Blake?"

Lori wrinkled her nose and peered in his direction. After several seconds, her eyes went wide. "Holy shit."

"Exactly."

Charlie had no desire to turn his way, but like a wreck on the side of the highway, she had to. She examined his features again. His profile still just as chiseled and defined and masculine. The scruff on his face made his jawline more pronounced. If it was possible, he'd gotten even more handsome, and sexier.

As if reading her thoughts, Lori leaned in closer. "He looks even better than he did in college."

His jawline appeared stronger, his hair darker, and his shoulders broader. When he smiled at something Larry said, she knew. It was him.

Christ almighty. What is he doing here?

His gaze traveled casually down the bar when it met hers. Her heart stopped, and her limbs froze. His mouth gaped. She couldn't blink, couldn't think, could hardly do anything but stare. He finally broke away and lifted his beer to drink.

"Here, sweetie," Lori called from beside her and set her beer on the counter in front of her.

Charlie glanced at the bottle like she didn't know what to do with it.

"You should go say hi," Lori spoke in a soft tone.

Charlie glanced his way one last time. She brought the beer bottle to her lips and swallowed a significant mouthful. No sense avoiding him. That would be childish.

She wended her way to the other end of the bar to see him chatting with a guy ordering drinks. She hadn't seen Blake in eight years. She didn't know what she would say once she reached him. Her palms went slick.

The breath she took in did nothing to calm her wildly beating heart.

"Hi, Blake," she said to his back.

In what felt like an eternity, he slowly spun around. "Charlie. What are you doing here?"

What? That was certainly not the greeting she'd been expecting. They may have had a tragic breakup, to put it lightly. But after eight years, shouldn't their history be just that—history?

"Well, I live here. And it's nice to see you again, too." She couldn't help herself. Sarcasm was in her nature. Her arms crossed over her chest.

His eyes lowered, then met hers. "Hi, Charlie. You look well. You'll have to excuse me. I'm not in a very social mood tonight."

Is that right? "So, what brings you to town?"

He let out an audible sigh and scratched the side of his head before smoothing his rich chocolate hair.

"My grandmother had a heart attack. I'm here to take care of her and help around the house."

Her shoulders slouched. "I'm sorry to hear that." She wanted to reach out and touch him somehow—his arm or his face—but she resisted. "How long will you be in town?"

"Likely not very long. In fact," he glanced quickly at his wristwatch, "I need to head back. I left her sleeping, but I should be there in case she wakes up." He rose from the barstool, pulled some bills out of his wallet, and left them along with his unfinished beer on the bar top.

"Enjoy your night."

She stepped back to give him room to pass, and just like that he was gone, as if he couldn't get out of there fast enough. Her jaw slacked.

Frozen in place, she wondered what the hell just happened. She stared at the front door, then back at the bar. *What was that about?*

She strolled back to Lori, dazed.

"So, how did it go?" Lori asked.

"Um, badly. He completely blew me off. No warm

greeting. No *how are you*. In fact, he couldn't get out of here fast enough."

Lori's lips scrunched tightly. "Asshole," she said through gritted teeth.

"Yeah, seriously."

"I'm sorry, babe. Let's just get drunk and forget about him."

"Good idea," Charlie said as she raised her bottle to clink against Lori's. Good plan, except forgetting about Blake Strickland was no easy feat. She would know. She had eight years of trying.

Blake slammed the door of his rental car harder than he intended.

"Fuck!" he yelled to no one. "What the fuck was she doing there?"

His ears grew hot. His fingernails scratched the side of his face, and he stared at the streetlights. This trip, he wasn't supposed to see her. She was supposed to be in Lace. And he definitely wasn't supposed to give two shits.

Get a grip, he cautioned himself.

He took a few deep breaths. After fifteen minutes on the road, he calmed down enough to get to his grandmother's without incident.

The house was just as he'd left it.

He peeked through the bedroom door left ajar to find Grandma sound asleep. With the house locked up, he retreated to his bedroom, whipped off his shoes and clothes, down to his briefs. He entered the adjoining bathroom and looked at his reflection in the mirror. On the outside, he looked mostly calm. A sign of the professional coolness he'd cultivated over the past few years.

Inside. Inside was another story. Inside residual anger bubbled up.

He hadn't seen Charlie in eight years. In some respects, it felt like forever, and in others, it felt like last week.

Shit. She was beautiful. She'd gotten more beautiful since college, if that were possible. And she'd let her hair grow long. It suits her, he thought. He could feel himself getting aroused.

"Stop it." *Stop thinking about her.*

Departure to Chicago could not come soon enough. Being near Charlie was bad fucking news.

Maybe he should call Adam and convince him to come to Fort Collins early.

He scrubbed his face, not really caring that the water was cool. He grabbed the toothpaste and his toothbrush. At this point, staying clear of Charlie was really his only option until Adam relieved him and he could get his ass back to Chicago.

Christ! He'd been in Fort Collins two lousy days. His cousins would have a field day if they knew he was leaving so early.

He could hear it now. *Wimp. Pussy. Can't handle a little girrrlll, Blakey?*

Shit! He'd say he was in a rock and a hard place, but ironically that was the upside. Some of the best rock-climbing in the country was minutes away from here. A corner of his mouth quirked. That's how he'd keep his sanity, so . . . time to plan a trip.

Blake checked his email one last time and then hit the lights. Even though the temperature was perfect for sleeping, he lay there, staring into the darkness. The only thing he could see was the face of a brunette angel.

The next morning his nerves were on edge, and his grandmother seemed to notice. He needed to get to work. Sweat it out.

"What's wrong, Blake?" she asked with a wrinkle in her brow.

"I slept wrong. That's all. Grandma, I'm going to do some work outside today. The downspout needs to be repaired. And then I'm going to trim the bushes."

"It's supposed to be nice today."

"Yeah, I saw that." He shoveled another bite of eggs into his mouth. "What are you doing today?" he asked her.

"I thought I'd go outside and pull weeds in the flowerbeds and my herb garden."

"Okay, don't overdo it."

"I won't," she said as she rinsed her coffee mug and set it in the sink. "Oh, I need to help set up for the church rummage sale on Friday. Can you take me there in the morning? I'll be there for a few hours, and Dorothy said she'd bring me home."

"Sure, Grandma."

"Blake, are you sure you're alright?" Her head tilted to the right.

"I'm sure," he said and rose to set his plate in the sink and kiss the top of her head. "See you outside."

His grandmother's concern was touching. But really, there was nothing to discuss. Running into Charlie was a fluke. It likely wouldn't happen again.

Chapter Three

Charlie stood before the natural and homeopathic skin creams searching for the right brand of eczema cream. She sighed.

When her mother called, asking for a favor, Charlie had a sneaking suspicion something was up.

Charlie's mom told her that she needed to drop by the health food store and pick up some cream for Mrs. Strickland's eczema. Apparently Rosie had a breakout on her back, and in this case, she didn't want help from her grandson. Her mother said she would drive into town from Lace, but knew Charlie was much closer.

She sighed for the second time.

"Can I help you?" a friendly, homely looking woman asked from the side.

"Yes, please. I need to find this cream." Charlie showed her the paper with the brand name written on it.

"Oh, that's here, on the end. It's one of our best sellers."

"Great. Thank you," she retrieved the bottle and headed for the checkout.

Several minutes later, she found herself in front of Rosie's house. She'd gotten here later than expected. The sun had almost set, and the view was breathtaking. Colorado is God's country, she thought.

All afternoon Charlie could think of one thing—Blake. She dreaded seeing him. For the past several days, she'd successfully avoided accidentally running into him like last week at Catwalk. He'd said hello, but she could see his defenses were up. After all these years. She shook her head. She didn't understand it. He blew her off, and it surprised her how much it hurt.

She exited her car and closed the door. An SUV was parked in the drive. She took in a deep breath and made her way up the walkway.

She rang the doorbell and waited.

Blake opened the door, and his eyes went wide. "What are you doing here?"

"Hello, Blake. Nice to see you too. Is your grandmother home?" Keep calm, she reminded herself.

His eyes narrowed suspiciously. "Yes. Why do you need her?" His voice sounded only vaguely less defensive.

"I got a call—" She stopped herself. She closed her mouth and pursed her lips, and glared at him straight on.

After a few seconds, he spoke. "What?"

"Any chance you can dispense with the hostility toward me? Or are you actually hostile toward everyone?" She tipped her head to the side.

"Charlie, I don't have time for this," he huffed. "If you want to see my grandmother, come in, and I'll go get her," he said curtly. He opened the door and stepped aside, allowing her to walk through.

He pivoted on a heel and proceeded up the stairs in search of his grandmother. He returned a short while later without her, and said, "She's asleep."

Charlie furrowed her brows and stared down at the paper bag in her hand.

"What's that?"

"Your grandmother's eczema cream." Her tongue swiped her upper lip. What should she do now?

She raised her arm before her. "Would you please take this and give it to her? I can return later if she needs help putting it on."

He huffed again and grabbed the bag from her.

Her eyes rounded. "Blake, what the hell is your deal?"

His eyes narrowed to slits. "What's *my* deal?" He pointed to himself. "Seriously, you're going to ask me that? I think you damned-well know what my deal is."

There it was again—a big ol' bucket of blame.

Willing an even temper, she replied, "Blake, it's been eight years. Don't you think we've moved passed all that?"

He stepped closer, invading her personal space, and pointed at her chest. "You may have moved passed it, but I haven't," he growled.

He was so close, she could feel his hot breath on her face. She could barely move a muscle, but she wouldn't back down. She raised her head to meet his stare. His body heat fell across the whole front of her. At this range, she could see the flecks of gray and green in his blue eyes. Even in his anger, he looked handsome as sin.

But still, she wanted to slap him and say *Stop acting like a three-year-old and grow up.* Wouldn't do any good. This was a pissing match without end. He had thought she cheated—clearly still thought she had—and there was nothing she could say to make him change his mind.

She relaxed her shoulders. "Well, that's a shame. I thought at least while you were here we could be friends, go hiking and climbing, maybe take in a movie." She held his gaze and as she spoke, for the briefest moment, Blake's eyes softened. In fact, she was so certain of it that now the stern, defiant look he presented seemed contrived.

Charlie blinked a few times, turned to open the door, and walked out.

The desire to cry was stronger than when she'd run into him at Catwalk. She blinked feverishly and willed the tears to go away.

She'd been doing well for the past eight years. The first year had been rough, but slowly she adjusted to losing him. Now it was like every hurt, every pain was new and fresh. Dammit!

She *knew* she shouldn't have gone to Rosie's house.

Damn her! How was it that after all this time she still got under his skin?

She was the last person he expected to see at his grandmother's front door. She looked heavenly in her hip-hugging skirt and sweater. If he didn't despise her so much, he'd put on a full-court press to win her back—kiss her soft skin causing her to sigh, tell her how beautiful she was, how much he wanted her, and bring her to orgasm after delicious orgasm in his arms.

Christ! What was he thinking?! She slept with her ex while they were dating. That's something not to be forgiven.

A footfall on the hardwood floor sounded behind him. He spun around.

"Grandma." He strode to his grandmother in earnest. "Are you okay?"

"Yes, dear. I must have dozed off. Did Patrice come by?"

Blake sighed and shook his head. "No. She sent her daughter, Charlotte. But you were sleeping so she left. She brought your cream."

"Oh, I'm sorry I missed her. Lovely girl. Didn't you use to date her? Charlie. Wasn't that what you called her?" She said, looking up at him as an eager smile graced her lips.

"Yes." He really didn't want to discuss Charlie.

"So, why isn't she here?" his grandma asked with a lilt in her voice. Her eyes twinkled with concern and love.

Shit! How could he explain what Charlie now meant to him? Years ago, she was his world, and that world came crashing down like a bomb to earth. All their hopes and dreams exploded into millions of tiny, useless bits with that betrayal. Her betrayal.

He ran his fingers through his hair and looked away.

"Grandma, she means nothing to me now." Damn! That didn't come out right.

"What? No," she stretched out the word. "You were so close once. Talked about marriage."

He circled and made his way back to the kitchen. "I don't want to talk about it, Grandma."

She followed him. She sat at the table and waited for him to pop the cap off his beer bottle. He knew trying to escape this discussion would be futile.

"Blake Strickland," she started in a firm tone, "I am very disappointed."

He turned her way. "Grandma, please."

"I don't know what happened between you two. But it takes two to tango. I suspect you are as much to blame."

His face flushed at her words. He could not correct his grandmother, but she was flat-out wrong. His hand gripped the bottle tighter.

"Now, Blake, several years have passed. The past needs to stay in the past," she insisted. She exhaled. "And you were raised better than that."

His jaw dropped. He shut it immediately because he had no words to reply.

"I want you to think long and hard about how to correct this. I expect you to at least be civil with her." She rose, went to him, and patted his cheek. "I love you, Blake. Now that's all I have to say. I'll be in the TV room should you care to join me."

Blake was stunned, to say the least. He shook his head. When did his grandma become so perceptive? Maybe she'd always been that way. He *was* being a jerk. And there was no good excuse for it. Anger boiled inside him when Charlie was near—an irrational anger considering the time that had passed.

His grandma was right. For his remaining time in Fort Collins, he should at least be civil toward her.

Chapter Four

Charlie grabbed one more apple and made her way down the produce aisle at the grocery store. She had far too much on her mind to work that day. Her latest graphics project had stalled. Her usual creative genius eluded her. The project would usually "tell" her what it wanted to be, but nothing special came to mind this time. Not since last week when she saw Blake at the bar.

Then seeing him the night before at his grandmother's house. He was so devilishly handsome. Emphasis on *devil* because truly, he was rude to her. What the frick was his deal?

Eight years ago when Den sent him pictures of the two of them naked, she knew. It would not be an easy mountain to conquer. In some respects, Blake had a fragile ego. At the time, Charlie was convinced the truth would win out. Blake would see what Den was up to and dismiss it. She practically begged him to see the truth.

Well, it turned out, even after so much time had passed, it still didn't matter to Blake.

Dammit! She needed to snap out of it. The pain of seeing him, being rejected by him, being mistreated by him, still felt raw. And frankly, distracting. The emotion got in the way of work and creating a beautiful project her customers had come to expect.

Why should I even give a flip?

The past was long gone. She had moved on. Dated a few super nice men—nothing earth-shattering—but decent men nonetheless. She knew Mr. Right was out there somewhere.

Suddenly, loading the bags of groceries in her trunk, a plastic bag gave way and spilled the contents all over the pavement.

Damn! See, distracted. Remembering my canvas bags could have prevented this!

As she crawled after her minestrone soup, a hand reached down and grabbed it. She froze and looked up. Her eyes needed a moment to adjust to the sunshine, but when they did, she could see who it was. She gasped.

"Blake, what are you doing here?"

"You look like you could use a hand," he said as the squatted down to pick up her black beans and hot sauce.

He stood and laid them in her trunk. Why was he helping her?

She rose and looked at him, not able to formulate words.

"Is that everything?" he asked as his eyes combed the area.

"Yes, but you didn't have to do that." She furrowed her brows still wrapping her brain around why he was being so . . . nice.

"I saw you were having trouble when I came out of

Bradley's." He motioned with his head.

The shopping area shared a common parking lot, so that explained why she ran into him.

Still rooted in place, he lifted the few grocery items from her arms, placed them in her trunk, and shut the lid.

Say something! "How's your grandmother?"

Softened eyes looked back at her.

"She's good. I gotta watch that she doesn't get too tired, but otherwise, she's doing well." He rubbed the back of his neck. "Charlie, I want to apologize for my behavior recently. It was inexcusable."

She adjusted her purse strap over her shoulder and felt the crawl of hot blood over her face.

"I'm not going to argue with you there," she said in an even tone. "In fact, I would choose several other more poignant words to describe your behavior."

His eyes appeared suddenly aflame. He moved into her personal space and pointed at her, just as he'd done the night before.

"What do you want?" he barked.

The air around them charged. His stare shot daggers at her. She didn't budge an inch—wouldn't give him the satisfaction—just glared at him. Her heartrate skyrocketed, and she licked her suddenly dry lips. His eyes glanced down at her lips, then back into her eyes.

The words formulated in her head to scold him like the spoiled, little brat he was when his eyes and his body noticeably relaxed.

"Again, I apologize." Then without warning, he turned

on a heel and walked toward his SUV.

She moved only her head and, wide-eyed, watched him drive away.

"Well, that was unexpected," she whispered.

She inhaled, slowed her stunned breathing, and sank into the driver's seat of her car. She brushed her palms down her jeans. Charlie had to admit that little interaction was exhilarating, and left her nipples tingling. Her tummy fluttered.

Oh, don't go there, she told herself.

Thoughts of passionate moments with Blake could send her in a tizzy. Standing close to him like that aroused her. Even though he was angry at first, her body didn't seem to care one tiny bit.

Their track record for amazing sex was outrageous.

Prior to meeting Blake in college, Charlie had had two other lovers. Den, and the guy she lost her virginity to. Neither were exceptional. They'd each fumbled through the act, knowing nothing about how to *really* turn on a woman. And definitely not knowing how to bring her to orgasm.

Blake was made differently. He knew what to do and learned her body quickly, she always orgasmed when they made love. Even times when she was stressed and thought there was no way she could climax, Blake only saw it as a challenge. Man, did he rise to that challenge.

Her time with Blake was a blessing. As much as it tore her heart out to watch him leave, she was grateful for all they'd shared. All she learned. Because of him, she learned what love could be.

Reminiscing about the past was a waste of time, though. Even with his apology, she felt quite certain they had no chance of being friends.

She exhaled and stared into the distance. *That's a shame.* Blake was always smart about technology, marketing, and climbing. She shook her head. Her lips curved into a smile, and she couldn't stop it.

Driving up to her little home, happiness filled Charlie's soul. She was still so enamored with her house. She bought it without her parents help three years prior. She found the little gem quite accidentally and fell in love with it. A covered front porch with a wooden door directly center. Flower beds flanked each side of the steps leading up to the porch. And a large oak tree graced the front yard. When she finally saw the inside, that did it for her. Hardwood floors, a large fireplace in the living room, a huge farmhouse sink in the kitchen, she could go on. It was perfect for her.

She unloaded her groceries and inspected the spilled cans for any damage. She would need to focus on her work now, her project. If she stalled anymore, she was liable to miss her deadline. And Charlie did just about anything to avoid that.

As she brought her PC alive, her thoughts wandered back to Blake. How could they not?

Really, he was all she could think about, it seemed, these last few days. Images flashed in her mind about times they'd shared together, things they'd done while they were dating. Including the intimate and passionate times.

Then the images of his face when he yelled at her over the whole Den incident brought any happy thoughts to a sudden halt. The utter, bone-deep pain written on his face when he thought she'd cheated on him still haunted her.

She had to stop herself, or else she'd start to cry. She fought for control. The emotion lingered under the surface. She would never forget the look in his eyes.

None of it was real. Den was an asshole. She might never forgive him. Because of Den, her life had been changed. Forever.

She pushed past the rising lump in her throat and opened up her latest project. Charlie was contracted to create some marketing collateral for a sporting goods retailer in the greater Denver area. She lived there all her life; this should be an easy task. She'd been on the lakes, climbed the mountains, and hiked this land since she was old enough to count.

She blew out a breath. The job was a major coup. When she got the call to meet with them, she nearly wet her pants. She *could not* screw this up.

She picked up the client's file containing the materials they had given her so far. The retailer had provided her with an extensive product list, and, up until now, had been using only whatever marketing materials were offered by the manufacturers. Her project was to create a comprehensive branding identity to complement the TV spots they planned to run. Hm, it's easy for a camera to capture the *adventure* of outdoor sports. What would her approach be to recreate it in print?

Her mind strayed to some of the outdoor activities she and Blake would do while at CSU. She flipped over to her electronic photo album and opened it. Before her, mini pics of her and Blake living life in Colorado's great outdoors. Climbing, hiking, biking, and one where she had convinced him to have a picnic. She smiled at that one. He called it a *compromise*, that if he went on some girly picnic, she owed him. She'd made sure to pay him back that night.

She was a glutton for punishment. She scrolled through picture after picture, so many great shots, some rather intimate. And she could only smile, even through her watery eyes. She hung a while on a particular picture of Blake rocking climbing. It was taken from a reasonably close vantage. How did she get so close while they were rock climbing?

She scanned a few more photos when it hit her—they had stopped on a ledge of a mountain. They were close to the top, but she'd wanted to take a break. Blake had agreed to go to the next ledge and scope it out. What a brilliant move to take out her camera before Blake was out of range. The camera picked up the beads of sweat on his face, the flush in his cheeks, the flexed muscles of his arms. She'd captured a brilliant shot. The strength, power, and concentration became more evident the longer she stared.

The ideas began formulating in Charlie's head. She shifted in her chair and sat straighter. She flipped through several more shots, maybe hundreds. Soon, she started tagging some of the best, a few in which one could almost *feel* the action, the sense of adventure.

Geez! There were some seriously good photos they'd taken.

She flipped back to her working document. She typed out a few headers: climbing, hiking, biking, boating. Then, cut a ton of text she'd already written. The focus had been on the products, on the features and benefits. That won't sell jack squat.

Energy. Emotion. The Why. Those are the things that will sell sporting goods.

She copied and pasted a select few photos, and sized them just so.

Wow! This is really coming together.

Charlie worked straight through lunch and most of the afternoon. The ideas were flowing so fast, her fingers had a hard time keeping up. Finally, Mother Nature demanded she take a break.

She exhaled as she saved one last time and stepped back from her work of art.

She chuckled aloud. Insanely great.

She rummaged through her refrigerator for something to make for dinner. Not having lunch made her famished. She found some chicken strips she'd cut up and froze in fajita marinade. Chicken fajitas sounded good.

She stopped midway from cutting a bell pepper and shook her head. She was doing it again—thinking about Blake even when she wasn't *thinking* about him. They used to make fajitas all the time in her college apartment. Most times, they could actually finish before he had her, naked, and writhing under his touch. Hmmmm.

One time she recalled, she'd been hand-washing the dishes when Blake came up behind her, flipped up her skirt, lowered her panties to her ankles, and had his wicked way with her. He moved slowly and sensuously, and wouldn't let her stop what she was doing. Crazy man.

God, those were the best times of her life.

Stop it, she scolded herself.

She missed him. She'd been doing well, forgetting about him these last few years. But seeing him again brought it to the surface—fresh and new.

She wiped a tear that slid down her cheek with the back of her hand. Time moves on.

Chapter Five

Friday morning, Blake dropped his grandmother off at the church to help set up for the rummage sale. There was crap everywhere. People, too. According to his grandma, the church benefited greatly every year from the sale.

Blake shook his head.

"Are you sure you'll be alright? This seems overwhelming, grandma."

She flapped her hand at him. "I'm not an invalid. I'll be fine. They're bringing in lunch, and Dorothy will bring me home in a few hours."

He tipped his head and gave one last look around.

"Go do something fun," she commanded.

There was no doubt in his mind that his grandma was a strong woman. But one look around he could see, even a teenager hyped up on sugar and caffeine would be exhausted sifting through all that stuff.

But, he couldn't deny. The mountains were calling to him. "Will Dorothy bring you home early if you get tired?"

"Yes. Yes. Now stop worrying. Shoo. Go have some fun."

He smiled and leaned down to kiss her cheek. He had every intention of having some fun.

He hopped into the rental and headed for one of his favorite spots to climb. Not too challenging, with too many compressions and underclings. The place he had in mind would be perfect for getting back in the swing of it.

After he had parked, he took several minutes to touch base with the office. The company had three top people, in addition to himself: Roberto, his right-hand man, Patrick, the comptroller and Marianne, head of technology. This time, he called Patrick.

"Man, all's quiet here," Patrick said. "Nothing to report. As to be expected in September, traffic to the website is good, and bounce rate is still low."

Blake knew this. He had been to the back-office and seen the analytics.

"Good to hear. Was Glenda able to fix the glitch on the pageview reporting?"

"Oh yeah, she had that done Monday."

"Super. Anything else to report?" He had an uneasy feeling about how things were going, and talking to Patrick gave him the reassurance he needed.

"Nope, but when you get back, Stephan wants to go on vacation. His brother is getting married in a few weeks."

Blake rolled his eyes. "Yeah, I remember. I'll keep you posted on my return date. A lot depends on when my cousin Adam can make it to Fort Collins."

"No worries, man. Enjoy your vacay. It's been—what— four or five years?"

Blake chuckled. "Yeah, something like that."

As he looked at the terrain before him, he knew it had been too long since his last vacation. He hadn't realized how much he missed it or needed it. He wrapped his conversation with Patrick and tucked his cell phone into his backpack.

He got out of the SUV and went to the trunk. The conditions were amazing: moderate temp with low humidity and a light wind. He changed into his favorite slippers designed for steep routes and bouldering. He pulled the Velcro straps to lock his foot in. God, it felt good. The adrenaline began to surge. He was in his element. He took one last chug of water before he slid on some lightweight gloves.

With the car door locked, he headed straight for the mountain. He couldn't remember the name, which was odd because he'd climbed it at least a dozen times. Charlie would remember the name.

The thought popped into his head before he could stop it. Yeah, she would remember. Several times, in fact, she'd accompanied him on this climb. They had some great times hiking, climbing, biking. Almost every weekend, they would head out.

Her muscles started getting so defined, it drove him wild when he'd see her in regular street clothes. A sleeveless shirt or a skirt cut above the knee could almost put him in cardiac arrest.

The memories of Charlie were good, so instead of fighting with himself over them, he let it ride. It would only be natural—being back here and thinking of her.

He arrived at an over-sized ledge and stopped for a break. He threw back some water and scanned his surroundings. He used his sleeve to wipe his mouth. This was God's country. Where the trees cleared, he could see a fair amount of the Rocky Mountains. The air smelled crisp and clean. He inhaled again. Charlie would love this view, he thought.

He stowed his water bottle and continued his trek. Occasionally, he would hear other climbers, but generally, the area was peaceful and quiet. His thoughts wandered to work a few times, his cousins, and his grandma. Admittedly, he thought of Charlie the most.

By the time, he'd made it back to the ground level, he was drenched in sweat, and his muscles felt tight. It was good to work his body, to test its limits. He drove straight to his grandma's house; he knew she'd be home by now.

He walked in and heard her in the living room, talking to someone on the telephone. He knew he needed a shower, but he *needed* to eat first. He opened the fridge door and started rummaging.

"Hi, Blake," his grandma called from behind him.

"Hi, Grandma. I'm getting something to eat, then I'll sit and talk with you." He glanced back to see her smile. She nodded and took a seat.

"Can I help you?"

He retrieved a bowl of spaghetti and scooped a bunch onto a plate. He layered the sauce and meatballs atop. "No thanks. I got it," he said as he set the microwave. "Did you eat lunch?"

"Yes, dear. Two hours ago." She chuckled.

He grinned at her. "Time must have gotten away from me."

"What did you do?"

"Went rock-climbing."

"Oh, wonderful."

He fetched the water pitcher and a glass. Then he picked up his hot plate and set it on the table across from her before sitting himself.

"It was wonderful. The weather was great. I could see for miles. Worked up a little bit of a sweat." He shoveled in a bite. "How did your day go?"

"Fairly well. Most of the work is done. Half of us left, and the rest stayed to finish up."

"Do you have to go back tomorrow?"

"Yes, I need to work a shift from ten to twelve."

"Okay, I'll take you. Do you think they'd need my help? I can stay too."

Her eyebrow lifted. "Well, that would be great. Yes."

He took another bite and chased it down with some water.

"I know you're just now eating lunch, but I'd like to make a pot roast tonight. Is that alright with you?"

"Absolutely," he murmured with a mouthful and nodded.

"Alright then."

She continued to watch him, and he couldn't help thinking there was more she wanted to say. He looked over at her. "Is everything alright, Grandma?"

"Yes, it's wonderful. I've noticed that you seemed to have

had a good day. The outdoors agrees with you. You seem so . . . relaxed."

He felt relaxed. He missed being outdoors, plain and simple. He would get his fill as much as he could before heading back to Chicago.

He smiled. She rose and walked over to kiss his head. "I'll leave you to eat. I have a few more phone calls to make before tomorrow."

"Okay."

He sat in the pleasant quietness of the house. For the first time in a long time, he could sit and eat without feeling like he was in a rush, or had something important to attend to. Perhaps he never really examined how much *rushing* he did, all in the name of work.

He inhaled, and slowed his eating, now that the initial hunger pains have subsided. Well, one thing was certain; he would definitely look into making some changes when he returned home. He needed to include more fun and relaxation time into his schedule.

He cleared his dishes and finished the last of his water, and stared out the back window. Surely, a little more fun wouldn't jeopardize the success of his company. Everyone needed to blow off steam now and again.

The office would probably appreciate if he had more R&R. The corners of his mouth curved slightly. Yeah.

Chapter Six

Saturday morning, Blake accompanied his grandma to the church rummage sale. The place was once again bustling with activity, only this time it seemed more organized. He'd helped his grandma at a particular group of tables; mostly he worked the cash. He chatted and flirted with the ladies as he made change. He cajoled them into making purchases, telling them it was for a good cause. In turn, he gathered the attention he paid the ladies—with the help of a full-on smile—would help as well.

As they were wrapping up their shift, Blake noticed a woman walking toward his table. She looked familiar.

"Hi, Blake," she said beaming at him.

"Hey. How are you, Trish?" Her name came to him at the last possible second. Trish had a serious crush on him in college. Of course, he'd only had eyes for Charlie so Trish didn't stand a chance.

"I'm real good. How are you? What brings you to town?" She licked her lips slowly as she tipped her head and fingered her shoulder-length blonde hair.

"I'm here visiting my grandma for a few weeks."

"Oh, that's great." Her eyes twinkled.

"So what have you been up to these last few years?"

"Well," she smoothed her lipstick, "after graduation I took a job at Patterson, Breakway, and Humus. I'm also studying for the BAR."

"Good for you."

She shifted her weight to one leg. "So I heard you sold your internet company."

He nodded.

"So are you moving back here to Fort Collins?" she asked as she nudged a little closer to him.

Her flirting was sweet. And maybe he could be interested.

"No. I've started another company, so I'll remain in Chicago."

She let all her white teeth show and placed her delicate hand over his. "You always were so ambitious, Blake. I'm happy for you."

He believed her, but again, he couldn't help to think he was being worked over a bit.

"Thank you."

"I'm helping my mom over there," she gave a vague point behind her. "You should stop by."

"Well, we are actually wrapping it up here. I need to get my grandmother home."

"Oh," she pouted. "That's a shame." Then she bit her lip. "I have an idea." She pulled out a notebook and pen from her purse and scribbled something. She ripped off the sheet and held it out for him.

"Here's my number." Still holding the paper, she stepped a little closer. "Why don't you call me, we can go grab a drink. Catch up on old times."

"Okay." *Pretty unlikely.*

She leaned forward slowly and kissed his cheek, and whispered, "I'd love to see you again." She pulled back, smiled, and turned around to leave. He'd have to be blind to miss the way her hips sashayed for him.

He knew he could have her naked in bed tonight if he wanted. He tucked the paper into his front pants pocket. He'd think about that another time.

"Who was that?" his grandma asked stepping up beside him, her purse in hand.

"A girl I knew from college."

"Hm," she scoffed.

Apparently, grandma didn't like Trish so much. No matter. Anything he did while in F.C. would be short-lived. He had a business that awaited him.

"Ready?" He offered his arm and escorted his grandma out of the maze.

Blake followed Josh into Broken Spoke, a trendy bar where the music blared through the front door. He had reached out to Josh when he arrived in town. They kept in touch through social media over the years. They were fraternity brothers and pretty tight once upon a time.

"I need a drink," Josh said.

"Yeah, sounds good."

He followed Josh into the bar and heard a distinct laugh coming from the corner. Charlie's face glowed with amusement, sitting and laughing with her friends at a corner booth.

Her beauty was undeniable. She captivated him, and in a way that pissed him off because he couldn't get close. He was still unsure if she could be trusted.

"Here, man." Josh shoved a beer Blake's way and took a swig of his own. He called out over the music, "I talked to Chuck earlier this week. He said he'd probably stop by."

Blake fought an eye-roll. Chuck was another fraternity brother from CSU. Blake remembered Chuck was a hard partier. *So much for chillin' with beers and bros tonight.*

The music changed, and a screech of female voices echoed from Charlie's party. Blake turned his attention to watch half of the ladies stand and shimmy to an open area to create a makeshift dancefloor. Must be a really good song. Long hair and supple arms were flying about.

Charlie loved to dance, he knew that. Something seemed carefree with her tonight. More than he remembered. She laughed with her friends and sang at the top of her lungs. She was having a good time.

She had her hair in a ponytail that night, and he couldn't stop watching her when some random strays floated over her cheeks. She enchanted him to the point where he didn't see any other women in the place. What he did see, the snugness of her blue jeans and the way her hips moved to the beat of the music. He did see the subtle bounce in her breasts and sensuousness of her moves, even if that wasn't what she intended.

"Bro, where'd you go?" Josh called from beside him, snapping him from his daze.

Blake shook his head. "Just watchin' the show."

Josh nodded. "This place is hot tonight."

Blake knew he was referring to the inadvertent female entertainment, rather than the establishment.

Both men watched the women for the rest of the song—something about having a holiday—until they returned to their *tamer* activities. It felt surreal in a way for him to be standing in a bar, watching the woman he was once madly in love with, without her knowing he was even present. It was surreal that she was once his everything. He had loved her to his core, trusted her, wanted to spend the rest of his life with her. And right then, she was merely another patron at the bar, out to have a good time with friends.

A patron he couldn't take his eyes off of.

Suddenly from the front of the building, Blake heard, "Sig Eps rule!" as Chuck came barreling through the parting crowd to make his way to his brothers.

Blake refrained from rolling his eyes again.

Chuck loved his time in college, and might continue to live the college life even at eighty.

"Chuck-ster. How's it hangin'?"

"Josh. Blake. Livin' large." The two-forty, six-two linebacker grabbed Josh for a bear hug, released him, and wrapped Blake in his monstrous arms before slapping his back. He smiled from ear to ear. "Let's get some shots," he proclaimed.

Oh, fuck! Blake wasn't up for shots tonight.

"Three jagers, please," he called out to the bartender.

Jägermeister would not be Blake's drink of choice.

Now it was Josh's turn to receive a slap on the back.

"How you guys doin'? Man, Blake you look like a stud. Success looks good on you."

"Thanks, Chuck. I appreciate it. How are you doing? Haven't seen you in a few years. What have you been up to?"

"Got the best job, B-boy. I'm a photographer for Playboy."

"You are full of shit, that's what you are."

A boisterous belly laugh roared out of Chuck's mouth, and soon Blake and Josh followed. Blake knew in his gut, this was going to be no ordinary night.

The shots arrived, and Chuck handed one to each of his friends. With his glass raised, Chuck said, "Here's to staying positive, and testing negative," and he slammed the liquid into his mouth as his head tipped back. Blake and Josh followed suit.

"Dang," Josh coughed out with a grimace on his face.

Before Blake could say a word, a movement from his right caught his eye. Charlie and a friend had approached them.

"Evening gentlemen," her friend said.

"Well, if it isn't some lovely Kappas."

How the hell did Chuck remember which sorority they were from? And actually, Charlie was a member of the Kappas but decided to leave before her junior year.

"Chuck, Josh, Blake," she said by way of greeting. "You

boys seem to be raisin' a lot of hell over here. Care to join us ladies for a dance or two?"

"You're on, Jessica," and Chuck reached for her hand and led her through the crowd to the area where the ladies danced.

"You ready, Josh?" Charlie said looking up at him, grinning.

He shook his head and smiled. "Uh-uh, sweetheart. I'll catch you on the rebound. Take my man Blake instead."

She looked his way, and he could have sworn he saw a twinkle in her eyes when she smiled briefly.

"Alright, Blake. You up for the challenge?" She reached out her hand, palm up.

Blake noticed her raised eyebrow. She *was* challenging him—daring him to say no. He was no pussy.

"Bring it on, sister." Then in an unexpected move, he took her hand, raised it over her head, and with his left hand pushed against her hip spinning her around.

She gasped. He caught her, countering her dare.

"Ready?" Without waiting for a reply, his fingers wrapped around her hand, and he led her to the dancefloor. The hoopla from a next song brought the volume up a few notches.

Blake spun her twice more, then let her do her thing. Charlie worked her supple body to the beat, and Blake could do little more than smile. She was in her element.

The crowd was energized, the music blared. He glanced back, and even Josh nodded to the beat. Blake couldn't believe where he was at that moment. His life for years consisted of running a business and working for its success—his success. He rarely went out and let loose. He was competitive, maybe to a fault, and didn't have time to just blow-off.

And now, he moved with his ex, watching her dance before him, having one of the best nights in a long time. Of course, the low alcohol buzz helped.

As the music transitioned to something a little softer, Charlie moved closer to Blake and wrapped her arms around his neck. A light sheen covered her cheeks and forehead. He rested his hands on her hips.

"Well, you seem to have loosened up some, Blake. Perhaps being back in Fort Collins is good for you. Get you out of the stuffy Chicago air. Because, honestly, this relaxed, less-serious Blake is my favorite. And believe it or not . . ."

He tuned her out. He was mesmerized by her lips. Her full, pink, subtle lips. Why was she rambling so much?

He snaked an arm around her waist. She felt good in his arms. He leaned forward and covered her lips with his. She froze a split-second before she relaxed into the kiss. She opened her mouth when he stroked his tongue over her lower lip. Her tongue met his in a slow, sensuous dance. She shifted closer to him, pressing her body against his.

The kiss spread to his core. His body awakened. It had been years since they'd shared a kiss. And yet, on some level, it was like they had never kissed before. It was a first kiss.

But his brain caught up with his body and reminded him that was not where he needed to be.

He pulled back and stared into her glazed eyes. "You talk too much."

Then he smiled and turned to head back to Josh and the rest of his hopefully cold beer.

Charlie sucked in air; she was breathless.

Holy cow! Blake just kissed her—out of the blue. Her legs were jelly. That kiss felt amazing. It felt like . . . something she'd want to do again.

"Oh me, oh my." Jessica leaned close. "What was that?"

She licked her lips and looked Jessica's way. "That was the kind of kiss you hope for all your life."

"I'll say. Think you should go after him?" Jessica asked with her eyes wide and brows raised.

"I'll think of something," she smiled, and after a beat, Jessica smiled too.

Charlie turned her attention back to her dancing friends, but what she really needed was a drink. Scratch that. What she really needed was an orgasm. After a several-month sabbatical, probably more like a year, she needed more than B.O.B.

Her face was flushed, and she could feel the beginning wetness with her every move on the dancefloor. God, she wanted Blake. She glanced back his direction one last time. She'd come up with a plan—fast—because she needed to put this ache to rest.

Chapter Seven

"Blake," his grandma called from the back porch as he pruned the hedge along the back of her house.

"Yes," he paused to look at her. "Everything okay?"

"Oh, yes. Fine. I was hoping you might take me into town later. I want to stop by Gladys's to bring her the casserole, and then the fabric store."

"Sure. Give me another hour to finish out here, then I'll get cleaned up."

"Thanks, dear," she turned and walked back inside.

Blake smiled. He felt so utterly domesticated. After breakfast, he helped his grandma grate cheese and chop onions for a casserole she was making for a friend. He actually quite enjoyed himself. Being in Fort Collins was certainly a change from Chicago.

In Chicago, his meals were usually at a restaurant or take-out. Hard work didn't involve sweat; it involved a computer. Fluorescent lighting replaced sunlight.

There was something rewarding about getting dirty and sweaty occasionally.

He moved around to the side of the house with the clippers. These really need to be sharpened, he thought. He should bring them along to town and look into having them sharpened.

A few hours later, Blake pulled up to the antiques store where Gladys worked part-time. He carried the casserole and followed his grandma into the store.

"Hi, Gladys."

"Hey, Rosie. Thanks for stopping by. Well, hello, Blake. Rosie, your grandson looks so handsome," she said beaming.

"Hi, Mrs. Bell."

"Set it here please, Blake. I'll put it in the back refrigerator in a minute." She motioned to the counter.

"How's Suzette feeling?"

"Okay," she said tipping her head from right to left. "Ready to pop. Doctor says he can induce her day after tomorrow," Gladys said with a smile.

Grandma turned to look up at Blake. "Gladys is going to be a great-grandma," she grinned.

Oh, brother. Blake sensed the insinuation hidden in that statement. He tuned out the rest of the ladies' conversation and let his mind and eyesight wander the store. A red metal tricycle grabbed his attention. The vision of riding one very similar to that as a kid popped into his head. He smiled remembering his dad jogging alongside as they *raced*. His dad always let him win.

He made a mental note to call his dad later that night.

After a few minutes, Grandma looped her arm through his.

"Okay, Gladys. I'll catch up with you later."

"Bye, Rosie. Bye, Blake."

Blake smiled and waved to Mrs. Bell. Sweet lady. His grandma had some really good friends.

Outside, Grandma pointed in the direction of the fabric store.

"It's only about two blocks up, Blake. I need to find some ribbon for the invitations for Geoff and Patty's anniversary party."

As they walked, he asked, "You're making the invitations? Why don't you order them, Grandma?"

She glanced up at him. "Blake, sometimes handmade things look better and mean more than store-bought," she said with all sincerity.

Blake never considered that.

They strolled through the front door, and in an instant, he saw Charlie talking with a woman, perhaps the manager, at the front counter. Charlie glanced up at him and gave him a quick, closed-mouth smile before returning her attention to the manager.

"Go say hello," his grandma commanded. "I'll be in the back picking out my ribbon," she said and strolled away.

He watched Charlie for a moment. Her hair was pulled back in a ponytail like the previous night, when he couldn't take his eyes off her.

He meandered to the counter. "Hello, ladies."

"Hello, Blake."

He noticed the sketchpad before them and the pencil Charlie held in her hand. "What are you working on?"

"Charlie's helping me with some holiday promotions."

From Blake's perspective, it looked like she was going to generate coupons for Halloween, Thanksgiving, and Christmas.

"Will these be printed or electronic?" he asked.

Charlie glanced up at him. "Jamie would like to do both. She has a growing list of emails in addition to traditional addresses. Jamie, this is Blake, an old friend from college. Blake, this is Jamie, the store's owner."

A lighting strike of energy shot straight up his spine. For some reason hearing her refer to him as a *friend* struck a nerve.

"Looks good," he managed to get out and offered his hand to Jamie.

"Nice to meet you, Blake. We were just discussing having the coupon be dollars-off or a percentage-off. What do you think?"

He had a definite opinion, but this was Charlie's project. He smiled and shook his head. "I don't know. What do you think, Charlie?"

"It's alright. It's just an opinion," she urged him.

He blinked. "Well, I think I like the percentage option because shoppers are apt to buy more if they can still save. The dollar-off may inadvertently limit their purchases."

"True, unless we create a sliding scale where the more you buy, the more you save."

Now that's using your head. "I like that idea. And of

course, you could change up the promotion for each holiday."

Jamie's eyes went wide, and she smiled. "That sounds like fun."

The store's phone rang, and Jamie excused herself to answer it. "I'll be right back."

"She liked your idea, Blake," Charlie said with a smile.

"She thought it was *fun*." He leaned close and spoke softly in her ear. Her clean, sweet citrusy smell filled his senses. "I can think of many more things that are *fun* besides coupons for a fabric store," he wiggled his brows and smiled at her before he went off to find his grandmother.

He couldn't say exactly what had gotten into him. Maybe it was seeing her the night before, but playing with Charlie felt natural . . . exciting. The way her eyes twinkled at him, she liked it too. These next few weeks might not be as bad as he had originally expected.

Blake was flirting with her. Wasn't he full of surprises? The way he'd leaned in close, his warm breath dancing across her skin, sent a rush of sensation to the apex of her thighs. God, how does he do that?

Jamie returned and reviewed a few more details so Charlie could come up with a draft on her PC. She was about to leave, running out of reasons to stall, when Blake and his grandmother strode toward the check-out counter.

"Hello, Mrs. Strickland."

"Hello, Charlotte dear. How are you? How is your mother?"

"Good. We're both good. How are you doing?"

"Oh, wonderful. I'm sorry I missed you the other night. I appreciate you making a special trip to the house."

"Anytime. Are you better?"

"Yes, thank you, dear. Perhaps you can come over for dinner sometime soon," she suggested.

She considered the offer. Since Blake seemed to be on his best behavior now, she could probably accept the invitation. "That would be terrific. Thanks."

"Does Blake have your number?"

Her number hadn't changed since college, but the likelihood that he'd deleted it from his phone was incredibly high. "Um, I don't think so." She grabbed a pen and reached for his hand. Opening his warm hand, she wrote her cell number on his palm. "There," she smiled. "Call anytime with an invitation."

Blake's lips quirked at her words and his eyes danced with amusement.

"Perfect. We'll talk to you later, dear." Rosie made a few steps to the clerk and set her handbag on the counter.

"Have a good day, Charlie," Blake said as he followed Rosie.

The day *was* good, and it kept getting better. "You too."

Chapter Eight

Charlie awoke the next morning with a smile plastered on her face. She was ahead of schedule on most of her projects and decided to take the day off. She'd earned it. Some climbing should satisfy her.

She strode to the closet and fished out her slippers, gloves, and comfortable, stretchy pants. Next, she grabbed a waist-pack and filled it with a water bottle and trail mix. For the sake of keeping her load light, she stashed her single car key in the waist-pack and left the key chain, holding multiple keys, on the counter. She finished her egg sandwich, pulled her hair into a high ponytail, and went out the back door. She hid her house key and took only four steps toward her car before her car key had fallen to the ground.

What the hell?

She furrowed her brow and bent down to retrieve her key. After a close inspection of her waist-pack, she noticed she had a hole in the bottom.

She sighed as she started the car. Time to buy a new

waist-pack. She knew of a place not far, and on the way to her destination. They would have a good selection.

She meandered to the right aisle in the store and stopped dead in her tracks.

"No way."

The words came out before she even realized she'd vocalized them.

Blake's head lifted, and turned to look in her direction. A small smile pulled at his lips.

She strolled closer, resting a hand on her hip, her lips quirked.

"No. Frickin'. Way. How many times am I supposed to run into you?" She shook her head back and forth in disbelief, not that she was disappointed.

Blake chuckled at her comment. "Hi. It is rather ironic that we keep bumping into each other." Not that he minded. "How are you?"

"I'm good. What about you?"

She glanced at the gloves hanging from pegs in front of him. "Looking for gloves?"

"Yeah, I noticed my current ones are wearing and getting a bit old."

He selected a pair of mid-weight climbing gloves in his size and slipped one on. After moving his fingers about, he put them back and turned toward her. "But really, I'm just killing some time. Grandma is having friends over today, so I decided to make myself scarce."

She smiled and nodded. "I see."

"And what are you shopping for?"

Her lips scrunched up, and she made a waving hand motion, like she was frustrated.

"Well, I noticed when I was heading out today that my waist-pack had a hole in it. I need to buy a new one before I go climbing."

His eyebrows peaked. "You're going climbing today? By yourself?"

She shrugged a shoulder. "Yeah, sure."

Did she not understand how *dangerous* it could be to be out there by herself? "Don't you think that's a bit dangerous?"

Her adorable head tipped and her lips pursed together. "You climb alone." It was a statement, not a question. And she was right. He could say nothing more without coming off like a male chauvinist.

"I just think it would be safer if you were with someone."

"I'll be fine."

He crossed his arms over his chest. Why was she being so stubborn?

"Fine. If you're so concerned, come with me." She paused a moment, then turned about and walked down the aisle to the packs.

He bit the inside of his cheek. That wasn't a half-bad idea. He didn't have anything planned, he had a free day. He stepped up beside her.

"Alright. I'm coming with you," he announced. "Can you wait here a few minutes while I run home to change?"

She shrugged half-heartedly. "Sure, why not."

"I'll be right back."

A "few minutes" turned into forty minutes. Charlie sighed when Blake finally pulled up into a parking spot in front of the store. She had everything transferred to her new waist-pack and she was more than ready.

"What took you so long?"

"Sorry. I wanted to grab some sandwiches, so we could stay longer. Plus I got us some more cold bottled water. Hop in," he said as he motioned to the passenger seat.

She gave him her best disgusted look, but deep inside she knew he'd made a good decision.

He chuckled. "It will be worth it. I promise." And then he gave her his full-blown, mega-watt smile, and she nearly melted in the seat.

"We'll see about that," she countered. "So where are we going?"

"Let's go to Horse Trail."

"Ah, you don't want to be home until dinnertime." She really didn't mind being gone all day. She was excited to get out of her office. And equally excited to be with Blake. The kiss they shared on the dancefloor the other night played on her mind. The idea of him kissing her again made her stomach do backflips. She could only hope.

Before she could ask him about his life in Chicago, he

began. "So you're doing graphics work?"

"That's right. I branched out on my own about two years ago and haven't looked back."

He kept one hand on the steering wheel and threw a quick smile her way. "That's terrific. How's it going for you?"

"Good. No complaints. What about you? I heard you sold your internet company."

A little spark of something flashed in his eyes. She couldn't determine if it had to do with the sale of his company or the fact that she knew about it.

"That's right. Sold it about two years ago and started another one almost immediately."

"Congratulations. I always knew you would be a big success." She let the corners of her mouth rise because she meant it. Blake was hard-wired for success. He could achieve anything he set his mind to.

After driving about an hour, they arrived at the spot in the mountain range for climbing. A series of stacked mini-mountains, instead of one monstrous slab of rock. From her vantage, it looked quite manageable without ropes. At least that's what she would continue to tell herself.

"I did some research, thinking about heading here this weekend."

She gasped and laid a hand over her heart. "By yourself?" she said in a high pitch.

"Ha. Ha, Lucille. Yes, by myself. But that doesn't matter now. I'm here with you."

Oh, yes you are.

"So, anyway, there are plenty of good quality routes, some parts have a bit of choss to watch out for, and if we stay west, there are apparently better footholds."

"Okay, then. Sounds like a plan."

They each tightened their slippers, slipped on gloves, and Blake slung his backpack on.

Charlie didn't want to admit to him that it had been some time since she'd been climbing. She was afraid Blake would baby her if he thought she was out of practice and fragile. She didn't want to be treated in any way but as an equal.

The trail built slowly up the mountain, equal parts hiking and climbing. Blake mostly climbed alongside her, occasionally behind her.

"Smear that if you can't get a foothold," he called over to her.

She knew that, but nevertheless hearing his strong, reaffirming voice next to her made her feel a million times better. Her heart raced, so she concentrated on taking it a step at a time. *Focus.*

"You're doing great," he told her.

Maybe he could see the extra beads of sweat on her forehead.

They climbed a series of ledges, occasionally stopping for water. They were a few feet shy of what looked like a good ledge to rest on, but she had no good place to grip. Options to the right or left were out because they protruded in an awkward, unsafe way.

"Hang on," Blake called to her, so she waited until he came closer.

"I can't reach that next foothold, Blake. My legs aren't long enough." She kept her voice light to hide the fact that she didn't know if she could go on. This particular area challenged her and consequently made her nervous. To top it off, her muscles were fatiguing.

"Here's what we're gonna do. The ledge is close, so we can sit, rest for a while and eat. I want you to reach for the ledge, and I'm going to boost you up."

Oh, crap on a cracker. "You're gonna what?" her voice went up an octave.

"Boost you up. You can do this, Charlie. On the count of three, reach up with your right hand, grab the ledge, and pull yourself up."

Thank God for her gloves because her hands were now sweating profusely. She licked her lips, and her little heart pounded. She shifted to begin to reach up when Blake laid his hand on the center of her ass.

"One—"

"Wait," she blurted out.

"What is it?"

"Your hand is on my ass," she huffed out. It was insanely distracting. She couldn't think about her next move.

"I know. I'm going to push you up," he stated frankly.

His hand remained on her as the discussion transpired. She had a hard time concentrating on anything except his big, warm hand. The warmth carried throughout her body and felt oddly comforting.

"C'mon, Charlie. Let's do this and get some food."

Food. She *was* hungry.

She looked upward and refocused on the task, despite the cupping of her butt by a beautiful man below her.

"One, two, three," he called out.

She reached as he simultaneously pushed her derriere up, and she gripped the ledge with her hand. She stretched the other one while Blake lifted her foot. She lay on her belly and swung her legs up.

She made it.

Standing, she yanked the edge of her t-shirt to her face to absorb the tears that had leaked out. She blotted and blotted some more. She had an overwhelming urge to cry with relief. She'd never been so terrified, and yet now, so proud of herself. Her arms trembled with excess adrenaline.

Blake stretched his long leg to the foothold and hoisted himself up after her.

He stood tall and scanned her body.

"Are you alright?"

"Mmhmm." Her heart had only just begun to slow.

He exhaled. "Well, that was exciting. Were you nervous?"

Truth or no truth? She opted for a half-truth. "A little."

"You did well." He leaned forward and placed a quick peck on her forehead.

Oh, she wished he hadn't done that. That simple action brought a stinging to her eyes. How many times had he done that in the past? A magnificent million. She glanced down, working on her gloves. Now was not the time to be overrun by emotion.

"Thanks."

He swung the backpack off his back and tossed it to the ground. He fished out the wrapped sandwiches and two bottles of water. He handed her a sandwich and sat beside her to start on his.

Nothing could have prepared her for what she saw next—a turkey and cheese sandwich with sliced gherkins inside. Her heart skipped a beat, and her mouth gaped.

Blake's brows pulled together. "Everything alright?"

"My sandwich," was all she said.

The stunned look on her face told him he'd made an error in judgment. "Yeah? You still like turkey and cheese, right?" He knew he was already pushing his luck with the hoist-thing. She'd been nervous, but she pulled it off with flying colors.

He was so proud of her for overcoming her fears and pressing on, words couldn't describe. He actually wanted to pull her close, kiss her madly, and tell her just that. But he'd already crossed the line once this week—kissing her at the bar. Reigning in his spontaneity around her was paramount.

"Yes, I like turkey and cheese. And you remembered pickles on it."

He nodded. "Right. You still like that, right?"

The corners of her full pink lips lifted. "I do. Thank you for remembering."

He sighed with relief inside. She was actually really pleased about the sandwich. He mentally patted himself on the back.

"You're welcome."

He dug into his sandwich like it was his last meal on earth.

They replenished, and he started feeling good again. Charlie chatted more about her work projects and asked him about his business and Chicago. It had been so long since they could just sit together, casually and contently. If he were in Chicago, he'd likely be anxious to see how fast he could finish before he had something to do or someplace to be or someone to see. Sitting there with her was the epitome of relaxation.

A breeze caught a stray hair, and instinctively, he reached over to brush it out of her face. She froze for a split second, but smiled and went back to eating as if it were nothing.

He couldn't help himself. He loved touching her. But that was in the past. They both had moved on, and besides, he shouldn't let it move beyond friendship. Friendship was a safe territory to be in.

They finished up, and Blake stuffed the trash back into his backpack.

"How about we go a little farther, then we can start our decent down?"

She rose and nodded. Gloves back on, they continued their hike and climb, stopping to enjoy the view when they could.

Her confidence appeared to be building, but as the muscles tire, that could be a dangerous combination. No sooner did he want to call over to tell her to slow down, when she reached up and pulled, and the rock gave way.

Choss fell, and so did she.

"Charlie!" His heart lodged in his throat.

"Ahh!" she called out as she fell several feet to the ledge below her.

Blake cautiously climbed down to where she lay.

"Are you alright?" he asked as he crouched down, whipping off his gloves to pull her to sitting.

He inspected her, touching her head, face, and arms. Her arm scrapped the sharp mountain on the way down leaving a massive group of reddened scrapes on her right forearm.

"Ow," she muttered.

"What hurts?"

"My arm, but I don't think it's broken." Her face was flushed.

"Can you stand?"

She nodded, so he took her left hand and helped her upright. He brushed off some debris and noticed a small cut on her leg. Other than her arm and leg, she appeared to be okay. "Can you move your fingers?"

She wiggled her right hand fingers naturally.

"Looks good." Damn, he fought the urge to wrap her in his arms and hold her close. Watching her fall was the most helpless feeling he ever had.

"Yeah, I'm okay. I think we should go down now, though."

"I agree." He pulled a small, white towel from the backpack and blotted her leg and arm. "Follow me, okay. I'll help you."

She nodded.

Together they worked their way down, without incident. Finally, they reached his SUV. "Let me take you home."

"It's okay. Take me to my car."

She'd lost some color in her face. She was more uncomfortable than she'd let on.

He shook his head. "We can pick it up tomorrow. I'm taking you straight to your house."

She sighed and nodded in resignation.

Good. He had no intention of leaving her until she was safely home and in bed.

She gave him directions, and they arrived at a little house set amongst trees and few neighboring houses. It suited her perfectly.

He helped her in to remove her shoes and wash the scraps. Most of the bleeding had ceased when he applied a topical antibiotic that he had stashed in his backpack.

"Do you have any gauze dressing?" he called from the kitchen.

"Um. I think so." She started to rise.

He rose a hand, stopping her. "No, I'll get, just tell me where."

She pointed. "Through there, in the closet, third shelf."

"Okay."

He returned to her side with gauze, tape, and aspirin. He attended to her wound. The scraps on her arm weren't deep, but they covered a wide area. He worked carefully to cover everything, and she flinched only once.

"Do you want some aspirin?"

She shook her head. "Just some water, and I'll go to bed."

"Wait here. I'll get it." He poured her water. "Are you hungry?" he called.

Silence. Then she replied, "A little."

He returned to where she sat on her sofa and handed her a glass of water. "Let me make you something to eat."

"You don't have to do that, Blake."

"Let me . . ." He stopped himself from saying he felt a responsibility for her accident. "How about breakfast burritos?"

He noticed her soft brown eyes sparkle. Yeah, breakfast burritos were one of her favorites.

"Let me see what you've got."

She began to rise.

"No. I'll find it. Stay. Relax."

"Okay. I can help, you know. I'm not an invalid."

"I've got it." He didn't want her lifting a finger. He needed to get her fed, and then safely tucked into bed.

He scoped out corn tortillas, eggs, frozen potatoes, cheese, tomatoes, and some green onion. After several minutes of prep, he served the burritos and sat next to her at her little kitchen table.

"You have a nice place here."

"Thanks. I love it," she confessed as a smile graced her face.

"It seems to suit you."

She glanced around and nodded. "I've made some updates, and as money comes in, I have a few more things that need to be done."

"Like what?" he asked between mouthfuls.

"The roof is tops on the list. I think it's been years since it was replaced, and we had hail come through a few years ago. I want to have it replaced before I have any leaks."

His head bobbed. An inexplicable urge to want to help her with her house came over him. But deep inside, he knew Charlie could handle it on her own. She'd done well for herself over the past few years.

His face must have read something.

"What?" she asked.

He paused for a moment. "I was thinking how well you've done for yourself these last few years." *And what a turn-on it is for me.*

Her eyebrows shot up. "I've done well!" She huffed and shook her head. "You're the one who's done well. You should be proud with all you've accomplished."

He shrugged a shoulder and took in another bite.

"Seriously, Blake. I always knew you would succeed in anything you wanted to do."

He held her gaze for a moment and saw the sincerity.

"Thank you," he managed to get out.

She sounded proud of him, and perhaps it had been a long time that he felt that from someone, aside from his parents. Her words struck him to his core.

They chatted a bit more and finished dinner. He rose and took their dishes to the sink.

"Crap," he heard and spun around.

"What is it?" He came to her side when her face scrunched up, looking pained.

Her hand covered the bandage. "Oh, I wasn't thinking.

My arm scraped against the back of the chair. I'll be alright."

"Why don't you go to bed? It will give your body time to heal."

She nodded. "I think I will."

He hung up the hand towel, picked up his car keys, and made his way to the front door.

"Thanks for everything, Blake."

Standing next to her, and breathing in her scent, tensed his muscles. He commanded his body to behave when all he wanted to do was scoop her up and lay her on her bed before stripping her down naked.

"You're welcome," he murmured. As he leaned forward, her dark eyes widened. He placed a kiss on her forehead. "Get some rest. Lock up behind me." He swung the door open and pulled it closed.

He gathered she thought he would kiss her, on the lips. The look in her eyes told him she wouldn't have minded. He would have minded. He warred with himself, but deep inside he knew—if he'd kissed her on the mouth, he would have regretted it. Again.

He ran his hand through his hair as he strode to his car. He wanted to kiss her again so badly it felt paralyzing. He could distinctly remember the feeling of her lips against his. The way she opened up to him. Time after time. Their connection was something you find once in a lifetime, if you're lucky.

He pinched the bridge of his nose. Well, something must have been missing if she needed to seek out her ex, he thought.

Chapter Nine

Charlie flipped through the channels on her TV. Nothing looked interesting. She had too much energy bottled up. A restlessness surrounded her that made it hard to relax.

She knew the culprit: Blake. The dynamic between them since he'd been back in town was capricious and perplexing, and yet held an undeniable sexual undertone.

Two nights ago, after their rock climbing, he almost kissed her. She could feel it. So why didn't he?

Her mind whirled. She needed to get out of her house for a breather. Yeah, a drive. That's a great idea.

Charlie grabbed her handbag and car keys and hit the road. The road she chose winded along a mountainside. She lowered her window and let the night air fill the space. She inhaled the freshness. Pine and spruce. She would never tire of the smell of nature or its incredible views.

She realized she'd arrived at one of the first places she and Blake had climbed while at Colorado State. Everything she knew about climbing came from him. They had spent an amazing day together—laughing, talking, and before the day was over, they were one with nature.

A flush crept up her neck to her cheeks. And her female parts came alive with the mere memory of what Blake had done to her, for her.

She looped onto a road that would take her to a lower elevation and closer to town. She opted to take the scenic route, so to speak. Knowing where Rosie Strickland lived, she decided to drive by on her way home.

She pulled the car along the curb in front of Rosie's house and killed the engine to admire the place for a few minutes in the moonlight. Rosie's grandsons were doing a fine job on the place from what she could see.

Blake. What was she going to do about him? What *could* she do? Her head lulled back against the headrest for several seconds. She'd love a chance to talk to him, get him to open up to her.

She glanced up one last time before turning on the ignition. A figure appeared at the window and pulled the drapes together. A few seconds later, the room light went out. That had to be Blake. The movements were too fast, the silhouette too large, to be Mrs. Strickland.

Blake was turning in for the night. That would be her cue to head home. And she had a mound of work awaiting her in the morning. So why couldn't she turn the key?

Actually, wait a minute. This is a perfect time to talk to him. There would be no distractions, no excuses, no interruptions.

She either needed to go knock on the door and find out what was going in that head of his, or drive away before someone accused her of being a stalker.

She was crazy, she knew it. But with keys in hand, she slid out of the car and gently closed the door. She walked with purpose to the front door.

Wait. She could wake Mrs. Strickland.

A faint light from inside peeked through the front windows' drapes. She decided to walk to the back of the house in the off-chance that Blake was still awake. Maybe in the kitchen. Getting a snack. Or a glass of water.

She knew it was pathetic the way she looked for excuses. She should leave and call him, or risk making a fool of herself.

The little light over the sink shined, but it looked like no one was awake. She opened the storm door, peered in through the window at the back door, and rapped lightly.

The door moved!

Holy cow! The door was unlocked.

Charlie's mouth fell open, and her heart jumped a beat. *How can that be?*

She squeezed her lips between her teeth. What should she do? They probably didn't intend to have it unlocked. And now it was open!

She pushed against the door, crossed the threshold, and called out in a low tone, "Hello."

She stood and waited. The only sound she could hear was the thumping of her heart and the blood roaring in her ears. This could be breaking and entering, right?

Geez!

Someone would want to know about the back door, for sure.

She slowly crossed the house to the staircase, calling out one more time. Everyone must be upstairs.

Her heart raced. Excitement and fear coursed through her veins at the same time. She ascended the stairs, and could quickly locate the door to the front bedroom that had its light on moments ago.

Last chance—push it open or turn and walk away.

Blake lay in his bed enjoying the quiet of the night. Fort Collins and Chicago were as opposite as could be. Part of him missed the hustle and bustle of the city, his work, his routine. However, being back in Colorado made him realize how much he missed this place, too. Missed his grandma, his cousins, his fraternity brothers, and yes, even Charlie. Even though he didn't want to.

Thoughts of her overtook his thoughts about work. *Now that's a first.*

Suddenly he heard a slight squeak of his bedroom door as it pushed open. His head lifted. Grandma?

"Blake?" he heard a soft whisper.

That was not his grandmother.

He sat up and reached for his bedside lamp to click it on.

The soft light illuminated Charlie standing inside his bedroom. She wore blue jeans, a simple knit shirt, her hair was down—she never looked more beautiful.

"Charlie? Are you alright? What are you doing here?"

"Yes. I'm alright. You're back door was unlocked."

His eyebrows knit together. "Unlocked?"

"Yes."

"What are you doing here?" He rose. He wore only his boxer-briefs, but didn't care what she saw him wearing. There had to be an explanation why Charlie was in the house at this hour.

"Um. I don't know. To talk to you, I guess."

He stepped closer and tried to examine her more closely in the low light.

"Talk about what?"

She smoothed her lips. Her gorgeous full lips. "I'm not sure." She pursed her lips. "I should go."

She spun around, and he caught her hand before she could take another step. Her hand was warm and soft, as he'd always remembered it.

"Talk to me, Charlie. What's wrong?"

She looked up at him like she was searching for something.

"You're confusing me," she finally spoke.

"I'm confusing you?" His eyes rounded.

"Yes. One minute you can't stand to be in my presence, and the next . . ."

He stroked his thumb over her delicate hand. "And the next, what?"

"You're . . ." She inhaled. "I wonder if you're still attracted to me."

Oh, sweet Jesus. He felt his cock stir. How could he not be attracted to her? She was everything he physically wanted in a woman. He may have been hurt by her once upon a time, but his body would always crave her. Always.

He was at a crossroads. To hell with his better sense. He exhaled.

"Try me."

She licked her lips. Her gaze rested on his chest, and then scanned down his body. She was thinking of her next move. God help him. If she didn't do something soon, he would attack her and have his way with her, and not regret a moment of it.

She removed her hand from his. Then her hands clasped the hem of her shirt and yanked it over her head.

"Fuck," he murmured. She wore a simple white bra trimmed with lace. Her skin looked smooth and practically glowed in the light.

She dropped her shirt and brought her hands to rest on his chest.

His cock grew harder. He cupped his hands around her soft face.

"Yes," he breathed over her lips before crashing down over them.

Her soft lips and warm mouth were arousing, like a homecoming. He dove deeper into her mouth and tangled with her tongue. She mewled.

Her hands stroked his chest. "Your chest is beautiful," she breathed.

"So is yours," with that he reached behind her and unclipped her bra, letting it fall.

Her breasts pressed against his chest, skin to skin. "Fuck, Charlie."

There was no turning back, no slowing down.

He wrapped his arms around her body and, without breaking their kiss, brought her to the bed and laid her almost entirely on it. His mouth traveled down her face, her neck, to her chest. She arched her back to him. He laved and toyed with her gorgeously erect nipples. He devoured her breasts. How long had it been since he had tasted them?

Her fingers wove through his hair. He caressed and kissed her breasts for several more beats while his cock ached for attention.

He stood and went to work releasing her jeans. He grabbed the waistband, and as she lifted her hips, he pulled them off and over her ankles, bringing her shoes along.

She lay on his bed in nothing more than plain white panties. Perfect. She was fucking perfect.

He leaned over her mouth to claim her. He needed to claim all of her.

He held onto her delicate neck with one hand while his other hand roamed south. He slipped a finger under the elastic band of her panties and made room to direct his fingers to her cleft. He found her warm and wet.

"Ah," she breathed when he skimmed through her slickness.

"You are so wet." He drove a finger inside her and stroked slowly.

She flexed, and the blanket bunched beneath her hands.

He circled her clit burgeoning from her delicate folds.

"Blake," she whimpered.

"Charlie, the minute these panties come off you, I'm going to fuck you. I won't be gentle. I crave your body too much. I will be a madman. Do you understand?"

He continued his ministrations. He wanted to see her come. Had to see her come.

She feverously nodded.

He thrust two fingers inside her. With his other hand, he yanked her panties off, damn near ripping them. Then he spread her beautiful legs.

He had to taste her. This may be his only chance.

He trailed his tongue down her sexy body, dipping into her navel before landing on her delicious pussy.

She trimmed her hair shorter than he'd remembered from college, and he loved it. His fingers continued a slow stroking of her core. Her breathing accelerated. He knew her climax was close.

His tongue grazed over her clit. She bowed off the bed. He glanced up and saw her hardened nipples looking delicious, but he would not leave his spot. He wouldn't stop until she came all over him.

She moaned. "Ah. Oh God, Blake."

He loved hearing her call his name when they made love.

He circled her hot clit and added more pressure. Suddenly, she cried out and slammed her hand over her mouth as she whimpered. He wanted to laugh.

Before she fully came down, he rose and removed his fingers. He wiped the excess cum from his face and pulled off his briefs. He lifted both her legs and placed them on his shoulders. With little more preparation, he held his aching cock in his hand, aligned with her delectable pussy, and drove home.

She whimpered and moaned. She was holding back, and he knew it. "Let me hear you, Charlie."

She shook her head against the mattress.

"My grandma can't hear a thing. Plus she's out like a light."

He pumped harder, and his breathing ratcheted higher. He groaned at the sensations of warm, wet Charlie enveloping him. Shit, how long had it been?

Fuck! He stopped. Her eyes flew open. "Charlie, I'm bareback. Please tell me you're on the pill."

Her doe eyes beckoned him. "I am. Please don't stop, Blake. I've missed this."

So had he. Absolutely no doubt about it.

His hips moved, and he leaned forward to cover her mouth with his. Her hands roamed his face, down his body and landed on his bare ass. Her nails dug in, and he didn't care.

He wanted her to come again, but he didn't know how much longer he could hold out. He changed his angle slightly, and she broke the kiss to cry out.

"Blake," she panted. "Blake."

Oh yeah. That did it.

"Charlie, I fucking love your body."

He pounded several more times, and the floodgates opened for both of them. She called out, and he grunted with the best damn orgasm of his life.

He gazed upon her sated glowing, rosy face before he pulled out to fall on the bed beside her.

His breathing brought in a fresh wave of oxygen to his

brain. What the hell was that, he thought. That was so right, and yet so wrong. Tension rolled over his body. The realization of what happened began to sink in. He *could not* get tangled up with Charlie again.

Been there, done that, and he had the scars to prove it.

"That was amazing, Blake," she whispered.

And how could he have used the word *love*? Granted not in a relationship context, but still.

"Yeah. Unexpected, but I know how you like to jump back into bed with your exes."

The words flew out of his mouth before he could pull them back. She tensed, and the air around them changed in an instant.

Her eyes blinked as she sat upright and stared down at him. "Please tell me I didn't hear that right."

He willed his heartrate to slow. "It's alright. I'm always up for a good roll in the hay."

Her mouth gaped, and sadness crossed her face telling him he went too far.

She stood and grabbed her t-shirt, yanking it over her head. She reached for her jeans and pulled them on just as quickly.

"Hey," he said as he sat up. "You don't have to go."

Her eyes narrowed at him with a glare that would make Attila the Hun cower. "Oh, yes I do."

She crammed her feet in her shoes and grabbed her underthings as she raced for the door.

Shit, she's fast. I better let her go, he thought. He may or may not have meant the words, but getting back into any type of relationship with Charlie was not a good idea. Not if he treasured his sanity. And his pride.

Charlie fled Mrs. Strickland's house so fast, she only prayed she headed in the right direction. She fished her car keys out of her pocket and started the car. Her mouth hung open, trying to take in a much-needed breath. She pushed some hair out of her face, and maintained control as she carefully pulled onto the road. She managed to get half a mile down the road before a loud sob escaped. She covered her mouth to stifle her crying.

What an asshole!

It served her right. She let some irrational side of her brain dictate her actions tonight. Blake would never forgive her for her perceived cheating. He may have been attracted to her, but it didn't matter. Tears streamed down her cheeks unceasingly.

How had she let herself walk into that?

Love, that's how. *Face it, Charlie, you've never stopped loving him.*

That's what the night was all about—seeing if he still loved her. If there was a chance of resurrecting what they once had.

Another sob slipped passed her lips. She had her answer.

Oh, but how sexy he looked. How good he'd felt under her hands, over her body. How could she have misread those kisses? Kisses that tasted of desperation. A desperation she'd never felt with Blake until that night.

Since their breakup eight years ago, she'd dreamed about his kisses, could replay any one of them at any time from their dating history. Never, ever, had it been like that.

She wiped her nose with her hand.

Damn him! Damn him!

He just broke her heart all over again. Will the love she had for him ever die? *Ever!*

Chapter Ten

Blake swung his legs over the side of the bed and rubbed his eyes with the heels of his hands. The crappiest sleep of all-time had passed. He needed to face what he let happen. A smart man would have seen his ex at the door and sent her away. Maybe said something like, *Sweetheart, our time has come and gone. If I've misled you in any way, I apologize, but nothing is going happen between us.*

Yes, that's what a *smart* man would have done.

Blake let his dick do the thinking for him last night. And the hurtful words he'd said to Charlie— Well, no wonder he slept like shit. It was called guilt.

As he reached down to retrieve his sweatpants and t-shirt, a reminder of the night before stared back at him. Charlie's white panties lay several feet away on the floor. She must have dropped them in her rush out the door.

He leaned down and took them in his hand. He couldn't resist their appeal. He raised them to his face. Her sweet smell hung on the white cotton causing him to stir deep inside.

Charlie may regret her decision to come over last night, but it's unlikely that he ever will. He should have handled things differently at the end, but Charlie in his bed would never be bad.

Her skin, her smell, her kiss, the way she touched his body—it all made him feel alive. The most alive he'd felt his entire life.

He did his business in the bathroom and headed to the kitchen. "Good morning, grandma," he said as he reached for the coffee pot, trying to hide how he felt.

"Good morning, Blake." Her head tipped to the side. "You look like you had a rough night."

"A bit." He grumbled.

Her lips pulled to the side. "You remind me of your grandfather."

He peered her way.

"Whenever something wasn't right, and it weighed heavily on his mind, he'd have a lousy sleep." She released a breath. "Blake, I don't know what you're struggling with, but you can't ignore it. You need to fix it."

She looked a moment longer, then in Grandma's typical manner, she patted him on the cheek and changed the subject. "Today, would you take a look at my bathroom sink? The faucet is dripping."

"Sure, Grandma."

"Also, tomorrow morning, I have an appointment with my cardiologist. Would you please take me?"

"Of course." He knew she could drive, but frankly he didn't mind playing chauffeur to her. Maybe he'd even take her Jeep.

His cell phone rang in his pocket. The screen showed it was the bookkeeping firm he'd recently hired to do the company's books. As business grew. Patrick got busier and more frazzled than usual. Blake was concerned he'd overwhelmed Patrick. Outsourcing some tasks seemed like an excellent option.

"Blake Strickland."

"Blake. Hello. George McAnally here."

"Hi, George. How's everything going?"

"That's what I wanted to talk to you about. I'm seeing some strange items, anomalies, listed in accounts payable." He heard a sigh come over the line. "It's likely nothing, but I wanted to let you know as quickly as possible."

"I appreciate it. What are we looking at here?"

"We won't know anything for sure until we finish the audit."

He felt the heat of anger crawl up his spine like a rat in search of food. George thought someone was stealing from him. "Dammit!" he muttered.

"Don't beat yourself up, Blake. It could be nothing. I'll call you as soon as we get confirmation."

"Okay. Thanks, George. I appreciate the heads up."

Blake stared into space. Could it be Patrick? It had to be a mistake. Patrick had access to the company's financial data, *and* the bank account. The balance sheet always zeroed out, as it should. He hoped to hell George was mistaken.

He took in a breath through gritted teeth. Could this day get any worse?

Blake entered his grandma's bathroom and thought he'd stepped back into the 1950s. Everywhere he looked he saw pink. Pink shower, pink tile halfway up the wall and the same pink tiles on the countertop. Oh, Lord. Grandma even had a pink toilet. The floor was black and white, or at least it had been at one time.

"Uh, Grandma. This room needs more help than fixing a leaky faucet."

She glanced around, like she hadn't seen the space every day of her adult life, and waved her hand. "Oh, don't worry about it, dear. We have bigger fish to fry."

Yes, well, this isn't staying this way for long.

Blake exhaled and leaned forward to set the toolbox down.

He reached below and shut off the hot and cold water valves, then he removed the handles. The corner of his mouth rose when he caught sight of a crescent wrench in the toolbox. Most likely a recent acquisition from one of his cousins. He pulled out the cartridge and jimmied out the ring and spring.

"Grandma, I'll be right back. I will need to get replacement parts at Bradley's."

"Okay, dear," she called back.

Blake had a hard time shaking off the funk he was in. On his drive to the hardware store, he decided to call Ty and Jack to see if they wanted to get together. If he could get his mind off Charlie, maybe things could return to normal.

"Hey, Jack. How's it hangin'?"

"Long and hairy and hard to carry. What's up, my man? How's grandma?"

"She's doing great. I'm callin' to see if you would be up for Saturday's football game."

"Definitely. We play Northern Colorado."

Hearing Jack's enthusiasm already started turning Blake's mood around. "Great. I'll call Ty, too. I haven't seen him yet."

"Excellent."

"Let's meet at the house. I'll text you the details."

He disconnected the line and called Ty. Ty sounded good, and he'd made a full recovery. So with plans solidified, Blake had something to look forward to.

He parked in the parking lot behind Bradley's and made his way to the building. He mentally went through the list of other things he would need for the house, like caulk and weather-stripping. He'd likely track down a few more things while he shopped.

Blake had immersed himself in his thoughts so deeply that he almost missed seeing Charlie exit a coffeehouse two doors down. She didn't miss him, though. When he looked over, she held his gaze momentarily and then looked away. She didn't smile. The coolness in her eyes and severity of her mouth let him know she hadn't begun to forget what he'd said the previous night.

He should apologize. He knew it.

"Charlie," he called out.

She opened her car door. If she heard him, she didn't let on.

"Charlie!" He pumped his arms to jog faster.

Her car door closed. She glanced briefly over her shoulder looking at him square in the eyes and took off out of the parking spot completely ignoring his call. He stood there watching her leave, feeling like an ass.

He wiped a hand over his brow a few times. He really was an ass, and a part of him twisted deep inside at the thought that he'd hurt Charlie. He tried to justify his actions, tried to ignore that it meant anything since she'd hurt him years earlier.

He let out a sigh and returned to the direction he was headed.

She knew it. She knew it. Dammit! She knew it.

Charlie had dropped in to review several mock-ups with Jamie before the store's opening. She wanted to get in and out, and get back to her home office, but that damn coffee called to her. Coffee should be outlawed.

Hot coffee in hand, she walked to her car and happened to notice Blake. He was hard to miss. He looked sexy as sin. His long legs ate up the blacktop. She may have stared a bit too long because as she watched his ass move she flashed back to cupping that glorious, firm ass the night before.

And then he had to ruin it.

When he spotted her, her heart stopped. She couldn't see him or talk to him for fear she would start crying all over again. Really, how many tears should one woman shed over a man?

The true saving grace—Blake looked like hell. The bags under his eyes told her his sleep was like hers—crappy.

Good! Served him right.

She'd keep the anger close. Anger concealed the pain of a broken heart. When was he leaving Fort Collins? She didn't know how much more of this shit she could take.

Chapter Eleven

B lake walked out to the porch as Jack drove up Grandma's driveway in his black Chevy pickup.

"Yo." He nodded to Blake and strolled across the front grass.

"Hey, man," Blake called to him. He hugged his cousin, feeling the sting of his hand slap on his back.

Jack wasted no time in throwing out a dig. "Are you taking care of some things around here or are you too busy staring at your PC?"

"You look like you peaked in middle school." He tossed back.

"Original. You look like—" He sneezed. Clearly faking it. "Excuse me, I'm allergic to stupidity."

"Hardy har."

Before the antics could continue, Ty arrived in a gorgeous '57 Corvette and sporting a brand new Rams sweatshirt. As he unfolded himself from the enviable machine, Jack chided, "Do you wipe that thing with a diaper?"

"As a matter of fact, I do."

He shook his head. "Blake, we'd better stop somewhere and get this boy some drawers then."

Blake rolled his eyes.

Ty grinned. "Oh, he's on a roll today." He leaned in to hug his cousins.

Grandma came out to the porch and greeted them. They each said their hellos and bent to hug and kiss her. From the glow and smile on her face, anyone could see how much she loved having her grandsons near.

"Will you boys be back for dinner?" she asked as her eyebrows rose.

Blake wanted to chuckle over the fact that his grandma still called them "boys".

"I don't know, Grandma," Blake supplied.

"Oh, well, I'll keep my fingers crossed." She paused. "And invite the girls, too."

Ty nodded. "Okay. I'd need to check with Faith, make sure we don't have plans."

"I could call Mya," Jack said as he shrugged a shoulder.

Blake had a sinking feeling in the pit of his stomach—the conversation was treading dangerous territory.

She looked up at him. "You call Charlotte, too," Grandma said as she clapped her hands together in front of her and her eyes twinkled.

Both of his cousins' heads snapped in his direction, as if they just heard some unbelievable news. "Um. Okay, Grandma. I'll call her." He knew his words were a lie. "But that's if we make it back in time."

"Sure, sure. Well, I don't want to keep you. Call me later. Have a good time, boys."

Man, his grandmother was persistent.

During the ride to the stadium, no one brought up the topic of Charlie . . . but Blake knew his cousins. He wasn't off the hook; it was just a matter of time.

After they had arrived at the stadium, they each got a drink and took their seats.

"Did you guys hear about the new stadium?" Ty asked.

"Everyone knows about the football stadium, man," Jack said with a grin on his face. Jack harassed him about how the new stadium was the talk of the town.

Looking Ty's way, he asked, "So how are things going with you?"

Ty leaned forward and rested his elbows on his legs. "Good. You know I'm the lead investigator for the Larimer County Prosecutor's Office, and that's going well. Occasionally, I fill-in at Faith's rehab facility as a personal trainer."

"You guys are living together now, right?"

Ty's lips curved at the mention of Faith. "Yeah. She's great. It's going great."

"So when are y'all getting hitched?" Jack nudged.

Ty sat back in his chair and refocused on the field where the action had started. "That's for me to know, and you to find out."

The Rams' wide receiver caught the ball and ran twenty-eight yards for a touchdown. The crowd went wild. Blake and his cousins stood to cheer and high-five. The guy behind Blake let out a whoop that left Blake's ears ringing.

After the stadium noise had subsided, the conversation continued. "How's the school year starting out, Jack?" Blake asked.

"Good. Looks like I have a smart bunch of grad students." He nodded in contemplation. "It should be a good year."

"And how are things going with Mya?"

"She's in the process of scouting locations for opening her own dance studio."

"Good for her. And what about wedding bells for you two?"

"Whatever." Jack smirked and adjusted his tortoiseshell eyeglasses. "We're not talking about me. What did Grandma mean about inviting Charlie over for dinner? Are you two back together?" Jack asked.

"She's *trying* to get us back together."

Ty and Jack glanced at each other and grinned. They were all too familiar with Grandma's matchmaking.

"What's going on?" Ty's eyes squinted.

Blake ran a hand through his hair. He wished he had something stronger than soda at this point. "I don't know. It's weird. It's like Charlie wants to get back together," he said while looking at the game, and not really watching.

"Why would she think that? Did ya' sleep with her?" Jack asked blatantly.

"Shit, Jack."

"You guys had a bad breakup, if I recall correctly. Has that been rectified?" Ty asked.

Blake shrugged a shoulder.

"That means no," Jack offered. "So, let me get this straight. You're sleeping with her, she wants more, but you haven't gotten past something that happened years ago. That sound about right?" Leave it to Jack to pry into his personal business.

"I only slept with her one time since being back." *Two days ago to be exact.*

"Doesn't matter." Ty was right. It didn't matter. After the initial awkwardness, the time he'd spent with Charlie since returning had been great. He also knew he was attracted to her, but his heart or head—whatever—wouldn't let him get closer.

He scrubbed the side of his face. So much for having a distraction with his cousins.

So what should I do next, he thought as he let out an exasperated sigh.

Chapter Twelve

The whole dinner thing with Ty and Jack fell apart. All the better. That next day he had work to do. Not on the house, but with Charlie.

There was one definitive way to put this damn mess with Charlie to rest. Blake needed to track down Den Pallasalla. He dreaded the whole fucking idea, but it didn't matter. He didn't have any other option.

Finding someone on the internet was relatively easy. And for a person with Blake's expertise, it was as easy as changing a password.

Blake stopped the car outside of the simple two-story house in Lace Saturday afternoon. He strode to the door and knocked. On closer look, the place desperately needed a fresh coat of paint. *Dang, Den. Have some pride.*

In a beat, the front door swung open.

"Yeah," Den said before the realization of Blake's presence settled in. His eyes went wide. "Blake. Hey. Funny seeing you. How's it goin'?"

"Den, we need to talk—either inside or out. What's it

gonna be?" Blake asked in a calm voice. He truly felt calm. Their conversation was going to be straight-forward and truthful. Blake didn't need to rip the guy apart. He'd moved passed that anger.

"Outside." Den swung his head back and called, "Honey, I'll be right back," then pulled the door closed behind him.

Blake took a seat on an old wooden chair.

Den seated a few feet away. "What's up?" His voice betrayed him. He was nervous, Blake knew.

"I came here to discuss what happened at CSU with Charlie. I never came to you." He leaned forward and leveled the guy with a stare that told him he wouldn't be fucked with. "I need to know the truth, the whole truth, right now."

Den's Adam's apple bobbed with a hard swallow. He looked down and hadn't raised his head for a while. Blake's patience wore thin.

Then, Den's shoulders slumped. He began, and not a moment too soon. "Charlie dropped by my frat house with her girlfriends. One of my brothers dated one of her friends. She told me she wasn't there to see me and that they would all be leaving soon. But we already had several people over, and the keg was tapped, so it was easy for everyone to grab a drink before hitting the road." Den wiped his brow with his hand. "I brought beers over to her and her friends, but first, I slipped a Mickey in hers."

Blake clenched his fists into tight balls. The fury almost shot him from his chair. He wanted to plow into Den, and body-slam him to the ground. The bile in his throat almost gagged him.

"When I saw it taking effect, I took her to my room. I was pretty drunk and not thinking clearly, Blake." Like that was going to be some acceptable explanation for his fucked-up behavior.

"All I knew is that I wanted her back, and I saw that as an opportunity to try and get her back. I took off her clothes and mine. I set up the camera to take pictures of us. Those were the ones I sent to you."

Blake's nostrils flared. He sucked in a long breath. "Did you have sex with her?"

Den shook his head. "No, swear to God." He scratched the side of his neck. "I was too drunk to get it up."

Blake slowly exhaled. *That's something.*

"Is there anything else I need to know? Anything you're forgetting?" he asked still containing his anger.

"No, Blake. Nothing. I promise. The whole thing backfired on me. She didn't want anything to do with me ever again. She was so pissed. May still be, I don't know. At one point, I thought she was going to hug me, and she kneed me in the balls instead." Den winced at his words.

Blake bit back a smile. Now that sounded like his girl.

At least Den had the decency to look contrite. "Blake, I'm sorry, man. She did nothing wrong. It was all me," he said as he patted his hand several times over her chest.

"Alright. That's all I need to know." Blake rose, and without a goodbye or a handshake, he left the dickhead alone to think about how he'd devastated two lives for his own stupid, selfish gains.

Of course, Blake thought to himself, you're a dickhead

too because you never believed Charlie. He'd automatically thought she cheated on him with an old boyfriend of two years.

What was his fear? That he couldn't compete with their history?

That was bullshit. He knew deep inside what he and Charlie had she'd never had with any other man. She told him so, several times, before and after all the Den-shit went down.

Part of the blame rested on his shoulders. He knew in his gut, what they had had was real, and he screwed up not believing her. Their lives were changed forever because of *his* stupidity.

He knew the time had come to swallow his pride and face her. He owed her that, at the very least.

⁓

Sunday evening turned out to be a beautiful night for sitting on the back porch of her house. The sun sat low in the sky and cast the mountains in the most amazing shade of copper. She took another sip of wine. The unfortunate thing was that Charlie was still alone with her thoughts. Her thoughts about Blake continued to consume her.

She heard rustling coming from the side of the house. Her breath caught.

Speak of the devil. There came Blake, around the corner of her house. He wore black jeans with a fitted gray t-shirt that defined his chest muscles. He approached. Charlie didn't sense anger or hostility from him.

She took in air, hoping to calm her jumpy heart.

"Hey."

"Hey."

"Can I sit for a minute?"

She met his eyes, trying to read what he wanted. "Sure."

"I stopped by so I could talk to you."

"About?"

He rubbed his palms down his jean-clad thighs and looked her way. His eyes intense. "About what happened between us."

Shit!

"I went to see Den."

Did she hear that right? She thought Blake hated the guy. "You did what?"

He leaned in closer, resting his forearms on his thighs. "I went to see Den. I never talked to him." He shifted slightly. "Probably because I was afraid I'd beat the living shit out of him."

Charlie turned her head to stare out for a moment before looking back at him. He was going there. Eight years had passed, and *now* he wanted to discuss it.

"I asked him to tell me what happened. He told me he drugged you so that he could take those pictures, making it look like you'd slept with him, and then sent them to me."

"Mm-hmm." Her lips thinned. She should be happy all this was finally getting resolved, instead only anger filled her. Her face grew warmer.

She stood and paced away from him a few steps before circling back. "Isn't that what I told you?" she asked in a clipped tone, crossing her arms. Suddenly she felt chilled.

He rose. "Yes, Charlie. And I'm sorry I didn't believe you."

His eyes dropped. He looked as sad as she felt.

She moved two steps to stand directly in front of him. So close, she could feel the heat emanating from his body. "You let him ruin everything." Her voice flat.

Tears flooded her eyes.

"I didn't know," he replied softly.

Her hands balled up. Blood ran wild in her veins. She reached up and pounded her fists on his chest twice. His eyes grew big as saucers. "You should have known." Her voice rose. "You should have trusted me. Trusted us." She hit his chest again, and he didn't budge. She lashed out, and he took it. He deserved it.

"Yes. I was wrong. I was a fool, Charlie." His eyes clouded. "I'm so very sorry."

Tears streamed down her cheeks. Her heart threatened to explode from her chest. Nails dug into her palms. She hit her fists again on his chest and repeated herself. "You should have known." Another pound.

Blake wrapped his arms around her body and pulled her flush to him. He leaned down to rest his cheek beside her. "I am so sorry."

Her forehead rested on his shoulder. "I loved you," she said into his shirt. A sob escaped her lips. Her legs threatened to collapse.

Eight years. Eight years she'd waited to hear those words. She cried for release.

"Shh. I am so sorry," he whispered in her ear again. "Shh."

He stroked her back with his hand, still holding her close. "It's all my fault. You were right. I should have trusted you." He kissed her temple. "Trusted us."

Slowly, her body began to relax, and the tears subsided.

Her mind spun in a whirl. So was she just supposed to forgive and forget?

She lifted her head and wiped her eyes with a hand. "Thank you, Blake. I've waited a long time to hear those words."

"You're welcome."

Her brows pinched together.

"What's wrong?" he asked.

She bit her lip so hard it stung. "I just . . . I just don't know if I can forgive and forget so fast. I mean, it's been eight years." His back straightened. "I fought for you to see that Den was lying. I guess . . . I just need some time."

He blinked and stared at her without saying a word. His arms released her.

"Do you understand?"

"Yes. Yes, of course. You need time." He ran a hand over his brow and through his hair. "I'll go now." He paused. "And give you some time." He nodded and gave her a small smile, then he spun around and left.

She stood in the darkness, the only light coming from inside her house. Despite the insane knot in her stomach, she knew she made the right decision. He couldn't just waltz back into her life like nothing had happened.

Picking up her wine glass, she walked into her house and locked the door behind her. She was exhausted. She flipped off all but one light and headed to her bedroom.

Did he think these past years were easy on her? With time, she had started to forget—forget about Den, and forget about Blake and everything they'd shared. But she didn't know if she had it in her to forgive. That was a tall order.

She lay in bed, staring at the ceiling, waiting for sleep to come.

Chapter Thirteen

Blake sat dumbfounded in his SUV outside of Charlie's home. She'd had every right to send him away. The blame for the whole Den fiasco lay with him.

That didn't change the fact that her words stung. Stung like a sonuvabitch!

He started the car.

She'd said she couldn't easily forgive, and that she needed time. For the first time, in as long as he could remember, he wanted that forgiveness.

Motionless, he stared at her quiet house. If only he could make her see how truly sorry he was.

He turned off the car.

He couldn't make himself drive away. What now? Before he knew what he was doing, he found himself sitting on her back porch sofa . . . waiting. Waiting for what? He couldn't say. He just knew that he couldn't leave.

Charlie tossed and turned all night, so by six in the morning she dragged her body to the bathroom. This is all Blake's fault, she said to herself as she brushed her teeth and threw on her clothes from the night before.

How am I supposed to handle this?

Her head shook as she stared at the coffee, slowly dripping into the glass pot. The anger she felt didn't simply vanish when he apologized. It wasn't that simple. Life wasn't that simple.

She poured a steaming hot cup, added a little cream, and headed out back to watch the sunrise.

She took several steps when she halted in her tracks. There, to her left, lay Blake asleep on her sofa. He looked so peaceful, she wondered how long he'd been there.

How many times had she seen him sleep? She squelched the desire to wake him and tell him to go home. Instead, she moved closer and watched him for a moment. His big body overtook her little sofa. That couldn't be very comfortable.

His face was so utterly calm and at peace. The same expression he had for the briefest moment the previous night when he'd apologized. Holding her in his arms, he'd sounded so sincere.

If she were pressed, could she explain why she was holding on to her anger? What purpose did it serve? Wasn't she just hurting herself? Or was she simply afraid?

He stirred, and she instinctively took a step back. His eyes opened and focused on her. He placed his feet on the floor and sat up, scrubbing a hand over his eyes.

"Hi," he said quietly.

"What are you doing here?"

He examined his surroundings. "I wanted to be here." He shrugged a shoulder. "I just couldn't leave."

Her mouth fell open. "You were here all night?"

"Yes. I couldn't stand the thought of being away from you." He rubbed the back of his neck. "Do you forgive me?"

As he said the words, a sadness passed over his expression that made her heart ache. They had to move past this, and it was solely her responsibility to make that happen.

He was open and vulnerable, it captured her. She didn't need to hear another thing.

She set her coffee cup on the side table and straddled him to sit on his lap.

His eyes rounded at her movements, but he didn't flinch.

"Thank you for coming back." She felt a lone tear stream down her cheek. "I forgive you." She smiled. "And I'm sorry it took me a little time to get there."

His thumb gently brushed away her tears from her cheeks.

"I'm sorry about last night," she said as she smoothed her palms across his chest.

A low chuckle came out, and said, "I deserved it."

She snaked her arms around his neck and quickly kissed his cheek. "Thanks for coming back."

He wrapped his arms around her and pulled her close. "You're welcome." He placed a soft kiss on her neck.

They held each other for several long moments. He felt good being close. His warmth spread to her body, chasing her tears away. Chasing her hurt away. Fusing the crack in her heart.

Charlie smoothed her lips together. Her heartrate sped slightly. He shouldn't feel this good, but regardless of the time, he awakened her. In more ways than one.

He pushed back a few inches to look her into her eyes. "I trust you, Charlie. More than I realized. I hurt you, and I hurt us. Thank you for forgiving me." Then he leaned forward and softly kissed her lips.

Time had slowed to a snail's pace. He pulled back to look at her again, perhaps reading her mood. Perhaps trying to read his own.

His warm breath fell over her face. His dark eyes locked on hers.

Kiss me.

He closed the final inches between them and brushed his lips over hers. His firm lips were warm against hers. Warm and inviting.

God help her, she didn't want him to stop. Her lips separated, and he slipped his tongue inside. His tongue massaged and caressed hers. A shiver raced up her spine.

The emotional rollercoaster she'd be on was finally coming to an end. And this is right where she wanted it to end.

He cupped her face and tipped her head to take the kiss deeper. She moaned into his mouth.

They may not have many more chances to be together like this. She would savor every minute, every second. Before long, he would be packing to head back to Chicago.

His hand moved south, and she loved the feel of his large, warm hand cupping her behind. He pulled her impossibly closer, and his erection pressed against her body.

His body against hers felt heavenly. She wanted him like she wanted her next breath. "Blake," she breathed.

"I want you, Charlie," he whispered over her lips.

His hands unfastened the buttons of her sweater while she yanked his shirt out of his jeans. Her fingertips danced over the ridges of this stomach and up to the hard planes of his chest.

He slid the sweater off her shoulders, and his mouth covered the exposed skin on her right shoulder. He kissed, licked, and sucked before trailing a hot path to her breasts.

She loosened his jeans button and zipper and caressed his growing erection.

He pulled one bra strap down, then the other. She was exposed but didn't have the heart to care. No neighbors were close by. And the way she felt right then, nothing could tear her away from Blake's consuming touch. She yearned for him. Probably had for the past eight years.

He leaned forward and whipped off his t-shirt and threw it aside. She took in her fill of his gorgeous body—his muscular chest, rippled stomach, strong thighs, and gloriously hard cock waiting for her. The sight of him brought a flood of moisture to her nether parts.

She slid off his lap and lowered herself before him. His eyes glimmered in anticipation.

Her hands pulled against the fabric of his jeans and then his briefs, giving her access. She wrapped her fist around his wonderful cock and lowered her mouth. Her tongue glided over his slit before taking him in completely.

"Christ, Charlie." His hands cupped her head, and his mouth gaped.

She moved up and down, taking him as deep as she could. Her fist moved with her mouth. His head lulled back, and the groan from his throat was music to her ears. She tasted a drop of pre-cum.

She loved doing this to Blake. And truth be told, the longer she sucked him, the more turned on she became.

His panting grew. "Unh. Stop. Please." He pulled gently against her head to pull her back. "God, Charlie. I need to feel you. I don't want to come in your mouth. Come up here."

Passion emanated from his eyes. She licked her lips, tasting his salty sweetness, and rose. She reached behind and slipped the hook from her bra, dropping it to the floor. Then she undid her jeans and hooked her thumbs inside her waistband, bringing her jeans and panties to the floor. She stepped out.

"Oh shit, baby. You are the most beautiful woman I've ever laid my eyes on."

She loved to hear his words of affirmation. She could recall a million times he'd told her she was sexy or beautiful or a slew of other gracious adjectives. Blake never held back on his compliments. The thoughts, however, were bittersweet. She may never hear them again after that day.

She reached to the end of the bench and retrieved a folded blanket. She flung it around her back and shoulders, and scooted atop him, sitting astride his legs.

"You are amazing," was the last thing she heard before he

cupped her face and covered her mouth with his. His kiss was voracious and hungry. She wrapped her arms around his neck and pulled her chest flush to his. They moaned in sync.

"Charlie." His hands roamed her body, cupping her breasts, massaging her until they found their way to the apex of her thighs. "Lift up," he puffed.

She shifted the blanket ends to fold under her shins and raised to a kneeling position.

In a beat, Blake's hand massaged her inner thighs, working to the center. One fingertip glossed over her opening, gathering her slickness.

"Fuck, Charlie. You feel so good. Stay right where you are so I can make you come." Then as his finger encircled her clit, his mouth claimed her nipple.

The sensations hit her from everywhere. She sucked in air while she clung to his shoulders. Blake's fingers stroked her lips and massaged her clitoris. He sucked her breast and shot white hot electricity downward.

"Ah," she called out. But that didn't stop him. He knew how to take her body farther. He knew her body better than anyone.

He moved to her other breast while he applied more pressure to her engorged clitoris. Her hands gripped his shoulder muscles tighter. She was so close, and then he slipped two fingers inside her and bent them slightly to massage her g-spot.

"Ah. Oh, God. Blake. Don't stop. Please." Her head fell forward as if the effort to keep it upright was too great.

"Never, baby."

He pumped his fingers and rotated his thumb until the tremors began and spread throughout her body. The explosion of sensation raced through her body like a shot. "Blake," she thought she called out, then sagged down over him.

He rained kisses on her face and neck. He smoothed her hair to the side to kiss her shoulders. His lips on her felt like heaven.

With both hands on her hips, he lifted her slightly. "Hold me, baby."

She raised her head and nodded. As she gripped his cock, he lowered her over him—inch by delicious inch. They moaned, and she took his lips again.

"You feel so good," she breathed over his mouth. All she wanted was getting him deeper inside her.

Hands on her hips, he rocked her. Their rhythm was just as she remembered it. All those years ago. Their bodies could work in sync, delivering pleasure together. They were made for each other.

"You feel so good," he parroted. He shifted his hands to the globes of her ass and worked them with his big, warm fingers. As he reached, cupping more of her flesh, his fingertips grazed her tight little hole innocently. She moaned not truly understanding the source of the sensation.

He quickly queued into her desire and brushed a finger sweetly over the spot several more times. She moaned louder. How is it this feels so amazing, she thought in her haze of passion.

Her pace increased. He groaned into her mouth.

"Baby," he panted.

He was close, but so was she. Even if she didn't come, she wanted him to come. She wanted him to let go, and she wanted to know she was the cause of it.

"Ah," she whimpered at the first wave. Blake flexed in time with her, digging his fingers into her hips. A small explosion detonated, grew, and spread to her entire body. An endless wave of pleasure. She was vaguely aware of his groan as he released, filling her completely.

Her body slumped over his. His arms snaked around her naked body, pulling her close. They reclined on the bench, naked, under the blanket, completely sated and at ease with each other. Charlie could easily admit it had been a long time since she felt so fulfilled and at peace. Which was strange in one respect because, really, it was just sex.

"Let's go inside," Blake said low into her ear, breaking her little trance.

She straightened to look at him, then tipped her head. "Why?"

He smirked. She toyed with him. Blake recalled times, after sex, when Charlie would play with him. A happiness would come over her, and he loved to see it.

"Well, I was thinking we could do more of *this*," he motioned a circle with his head, "inside . . . on your bed, perhaps."

"Well, I've already *had* this." She motioned the same way he did.

"So, perhaps you'd like something new?" He lifted an eyebrow.

"Hmm." She tilted her head, as if contemplating the universe, and a mass of long hair fell to the side.

He suddenly wanted that cascading over him, gliding over his chest, tangled in between his fingers.

"I was thinking I could lay you out on your bed and spread your legs wide so that I could taste you."

He felt a quiver down her back.

"Unless, of course, we don't make it that far. Then I suppose I'll have to take you on the kitchen table. I would make you come several times before I dove deep inside you." His mere words caused his cock to stir inside her.

Without waiting for another response, he rose, his arms holding her tightly to him as he negotiated out of his jeans. He stepped away from the porch, the clothes strewn about like a cyclone had blown through. He carried his soft, naked, warm Charlie inside and laid her on the kitchen table. He slipped out of her, with much regret.

"No," she exclaimed. "Blake, you cannot be serious."

Quick as a whip, he leaned over her, grabbed a handful of hair beneath her head to tilt her face toward his. She gasped. "I am very serious." He claimed her mouth in a deep, passionate kiss. He rather liked all this long hair to do with as he wished.

He broke the kiss. "You can cover up, just stay put. I'm not through with you yet," he said with a smile.

He walked to the sink and turned on the hot water. He rummaged for a washcloth and after the third drawer, he located one. It looked new. He smiled.

He wetted the washcloth and returned to find her waiting as he'd left her, her face flush, and the blanket wrapped around her.

"Put your feet on the table."

She hesitated briefly. He noticed she took in air, and her nostrils widened. Despite her tentativeness, she lifted her feet on the table, and he opened her wider.

"Christ, you're beautiful."

With the warm washcloth, he smoothed and gently wiped her pussy of his semen. He heard her suck in a breath. His actions were turning her on. He wiped some more and dropped the cloth on the tile floor before he pushed his finger inside her.

Charlie's back bowed off the table. He wanted to see her come again.

The sun was rising. The light streamed through the room and cast Charlie in the most amazing glow.

"You look beautiful." He whispered over her lips as he slipped another finger into her warm, wet channel.

"Blake," she breathed.

Her clit swelled more, in anticipation of another climax. Perfect timing. He wanted to make her come, then drive in deep. His cock ached to be inside her again.

He moved away from her face and bent down between her legs. He glossed his tongue lightly over her engorged clit. Slowly, he teased her with his tongue all while stroking and twisting his fingers inside her.

She panted. "Oh God, Blake."

He applied more pressure with his tongue. At the same time, he pulled out his fingers and pushed her legs down and open.

"Ah," she cried out. Her fingers wrapped around the edge of the table, the blanket long forgotten.

He worked her until she screamed his name, then he rose to enter her, hitting her end.

He fastened his mouth to hers. Her arms and legs swung around him as he moved in her. They rocked together, and in several beats, he released all his cum inside her like they hadn't just made love minutes before.

He was positively mad for her. He couldn't get enough. He'd barely caught his breath when he hoisted her into his arms and carried her to the bedroom.

He laid her down and made love to her one more time before he had to go. He wanted to stay all day. He shouldn't have wanted it so bad, but he did. Regardless, he needed to get back to the house to check on his grandma.

After retrieving their clothes from the back porch, he pulled on his jeans and buckled his belt. "Charlie, I have to go."

"I know." She sat upright on her bed; her arm holding the sheet covering her torso.

He leaned forward, his hands straddling her supple body. "Have dinner with me tonight."

Her beautiful white teeth showed with her stunning smile. Her eyes sparkled. "Okay."

"I'll pick you up at seven."

She nodded, and he clutched the back of her neck for one last long kiss.

He turned to leave wondering if what he'd just done was right. Having sex with Charlie and then making plans to spend more time with her. He wanted to be with her, but knew deep down it was a bad idea.

His cheeks pillowed, and he let out a long breath. They lived a world apart. Starting a relationship with Charlie wouldn't be a smart move. He shouldn't lead her on. He was leaving in less than two weeks.

Chapter Fourteen

Blake rang her doorbell right on time for their date. Butterflies filled her stomach like this was a first date. She giggled inside. This was far from a first date.

She opened the door, and found tall, sexy Blake standing before her. He wore a gray button-down and black slacks sporting a black belt with a polished buckle. Very understated, yet oozing style at the same time. The clothes fit him like they were custom-made.

"Hi."

"Hi. You look lovely," he said as pressed a warm kiss on her cheek.

She'd grappled over what to wear, finally settling on a LBD—little black dress—with sleeves to cover the white bandage. She worried if she would be over-dressed.

"Thank you. And you look handsome."

"I want to try a new place in Loveland. It's supposed to get chilly tonight. Do you have a jacket?"

She nodded. "Yes. Be right back." She scurried to her bedroom, grabbed her phone and shoved it into her little purse, and scooped up her jacket laying on the bed.

After a short drive, they arrived at a Mediterranean restaurant on the lake. They were shown to a corner table in the enclosed patio with an exceptional view of the lake. The moon and stars reflected off the water creating a sparkling glow. "Oh Blake, this is beautiful."

"I'm glad you like it. I heard good things about the place, so I thought we should give it a try."

"Good call."

"Here," he pulled out a chair for her to sit, facing the water and then took the seat next to her.

Immediately, she felt his body heat warm the side of her. Being out on a date with Blake felt comfortable and familiar in one respect. Yet in another way, it felt new and exhilarating as both of them had changed since college. A healthy dose of giddiness running rampant in her veins. Admittedly she'd been thinking about their date the entire day. And there she sat, staring at the menu, trying her damnedest to read the words to make a decision about dinner.

She peered under her lashes at Blake. He studied the menu intently as well and shifted in his seat to get more comfortable.

The waiter emerged before she could say anything. "Evening folks. May I start you all with a drink?"

Blake's eyes met his. "Yes. We'll take a bottle of Cakebread Chardonnay, and let's start with a shrimp appetizer."

"Very well, sir."

He remembered how much she liked white wine. And Cakebread made her practically orgasmic.

He set his menu down and faced her. "How's your arm?"

"Healing nicely."

His eyes glanced down briefly. "I'm sorry about that, Charlie."

She covered his lips with her fingertips. "No apologies. I'm alright, and it's no one's fault. I'll be fine."

His lips curved, and he nodded.

They drank their wine and devoured the shrimp. She couldn't help notice Blake seemed fidgety that night, in a way she'd never seen. Was he nervous? Clearly, he had something important on his mind.

He needed to find the words. He was stalling. The sooner he laid his cards on the table, the better. He licked his lips for the hundredth time. "Charlie, I need to talk to you."

She looked up from her wineglass. Her eyes hardened on alert. "Okay."

His heart raced like a jackrabbit. He wanted to be honest with Charlie, but not hurt her in the process.

"I'm leaving for Chicago in two weeks."

"Right."

"I want to see you, but . . ." Why was it so difficult to just spit it out?

"But you don't see us having a long-term relationship," she finished for him.

She knew. He let a breath. "Yes. It would complicate

things. I live far away. I have a business there. You have your family here and a growing business. We . . ."

"I know." She laid her hand over his forearm. "Our time has come and gone. I understand. I'm good with that. We have our own lives, in separate states. It's good. So let's just enjoy our time together now." Her lips curved. It wasn't a big smile, but it seemed sincere.

She understood. He should be relieved. And yet, his stomach turned hard as concrete at her words. *Our time has come and gone.* She was right. He knew it. They both knew it. They should enjoy the time they had together.

He forced a smile, lifted her hand, and kissed the back of it.

They drank the entire bottle of wine, which helped him to relax. The conversation rolled, and the evening was turning out better than he had expected. She laughed at his jokes, asked questions about his company, talked about her plans for her company. They ordered coffee and dessert and could have stayed longer.

"C'mon. It's getting late. I should take you home."

He held her hand the whole drive home, and she didn't seem to mind one bit. He needed to be touching her. When he pulled into her driveway, all he could think about was touching her from head to toe. Every soft, sweet part of her body.

He'd berated himself earlier. That night would be different. They weren't going to be fuck-buddies for two weeks. He wasn't going to use her and skip town. No, that night he would be a gentleman. He would kiss her goodnight and leave her alone.

And maybe that's why he held her hand. So he wouldn't touch any part of those vastly appealing legs.

"Stay put." He smiled. He exited the car and walked to her side to open her door.

"Thank you, kind sir."

She clasped his hand, swung her legs out, and rose. He was overcome. He pulled her close and plunged his lips over hers. He swiped his tongue against her. He could still taste the chocolate on her from earlier. "I love this dress on you," he breathed over her lips. "Your legs look good enough to eat."

Her darkened eyes sparkled. "Thank you," she whispered. "Would you like to come in?"

He was tempted. "Not tonight. I need to check on my grandma. Tomorrow. How about a movie?"

A smile quickly covered her disappointment. "Okay."

He walked her to the door and unlocked it. "I'm trying to be a gentleman here, Charlie."

"Okay," she said as she coyly peered up at him with an innocent smile.

He pulled her close one last time to claim her soft mouth, teasing, longing for more. His hand stroked her thigh. She moaned, and that spurred his hand to move higher. She hadn't worn stockings, and quickly he learned her ass was bare. He couldn't help himself. He had to know if she wore panties. Bunching her short black dress as his hand reached up her round globe, he felt her skimpy lace confection.

"Fuck, you feel so good."

He massaged and caressed her ass. She whimpered in his mouth. He should stop. His first two fingers slid under the thong to her mons and down her slit. She was so wet.

She wants you, said the devil on his shoulder.

No, walk away, said the angel.

He dipped a finger through her lips to her core. He lightly pressed a finger in up to the first knuckle. He broke the kiss, pulled out his finger, and slowly sucked his finger clean.

Her dark eyes widened at his action.

"Go inside, strip out of that dress, and fuck yourself with your vibrator. I want to go home and picture your luscious body, spread out on your bed, pleasuring yourself. Making yourself come. When that vibrator glides inside you, picture it's my cock. Understand?"

Her precious red lips gaped. She nodded.

He stepped back, and waited for her to turn around and walk inside. When he heard the door lock, he returned to his SUV.

"Christ almighty," he exhaled. He nearly hauled her inside, laid her down on the first flat surface he found, and fucked her until she screamed in ecstasy. He wanted her in the worst kind of way. But she wasn't just some girl, and he didn't want to treat her as such.

His cock was hard as granite. He shifted in his seat to get comfortable. He'd need to take care of this ache. Soon.

Charlie had done what he said. She undressed, lay on her bed, and used her vibrator. It took hardly any time for her to climax. When she was through, she texted him.

Satisfied, but only partially. I need another one.

He must have been doing something because his response took a few minutes.

Oh, no babe. The next one is mine.

She sighed.

She rose from her bed and went to her bathroom to ready herself for bed. Thoughts about their conversation over dinner trickled into her mind. She suspected he'd want to clear the air about not having a relationship, not wanting to complicate things between them. She understood that. She'd agreed to that. But she didn't like it.

Of course, it made absolute sense. They lived over a thousand miles away from each other.

She felt tears pricking the backs of her eyes. She finally had Blake back. They were free from the black cloud of the past that hung over them for so long. And she wanted him in her life. Was she asking too much?

Back in Chicago, Blake had a thriving, successful business. She couldn't ask him to give that up to move back to Colorado. *She* also had a successful business, and her family was here. She could leave no easier than he could.

She sighed and flipped off the light switch. *Enjoy the time you have, Charlie.*

Sure. Easier said than done.

Chapter Fifteen

Charlie poured the last of the coffee into her cup. Back to work, she thought. Enough daydreaming. Because that's what she'd been doing, daydreaming about Blake.

Until . . .

She thought about their date—a nearly perfect date. Except for the fact that he didn't see them having a long-term or long-distance relationship, it had been perfect.

She exhaled. She tried to focus on work because the knot in her stomach was distracting. She looked down at the coffee she'd just fixed and grimaced. She poured it down the drain and left the cup in the sink.

Focus, Charlie.

Her next project didn't require an inordinate amount of thought. A local insurance agency contracted her to create a retractable, floor-standing banner to be used for trade show and expos. She worked the mouse with placing a graphic, then their logo. She reviewed the text. Perhaps a border. Yeah, nice touch. She saved her work.

Her thoughts wandered. "At least he wants to see you

tonight," she said to herself. A smile tugged at the corners of her lips. What should she wear?

Her mind replayed the movements of his hands, his mouth, his hard body. That brought her lady-parts alive. Would he be a "gentleman" tonight or would he give her what she craved? What she knew he craved too.

So what if they only had two weeks together. Why let it go to waste?

⌘

A knock at the door snapped Blake from his thoughts. "I'll get it, Grandma," he called as he walked to the front door. He was expecting a general contractor, to look at his grandmother's bathroom. Or the *Pink Powderpuff of Plumbing* as he liked to call it.

"Hello. Mister Strickland?" A man with bright eyes, wide shoulders, and an extra forty pounds on him stood at the door with a notebook in one hand, extending the other.

Blake shook his hand. "Yes. Mister Harrison. Good to meet you. Come in."

"Please call me Bill. You'd like to remodel a bathroom, is that right?"

"Yes. Right this way."

The man trailed Blake upstairs where grandma sat at her tiny desk writing. She looked up from her work and smiled. "Hello, Mister Harrison. I'm Rosie Strickland. So glad to meet you."

"You, too, ma'am."

"Please follow me."

They walked into the space, and to Bill's credit, he didn't let on that he could lose his lunch at any point.

Blake started. "I don't think there is anything of value here that needs to be saved. I'd like my grandma to have the most up-to-date, current bathroom possible and still fit with the style of the house."

"Yes, of course."

Immediately, Bill started making notes and taking measurements. "Do you like the layout of the bathroom, Mrs. Strickland?"

"Um, yes. I do."

"Good. So do I. The toilet isn't too far from the door. Now, I'd like to create a barrier-free shower," he stooped down and motioned back and forth with his hand by the shower door. "If we take away this little step here, it will make it easier long-term for getting in and out of the shower."

"Terrific. I like that idea," his grandma smiled. Blake loved to see that smile. Just as much as he loved to see it on Charlie's face.

Bill and Grandma spoke about a few other particulars until they were both comfortable that he understood what she wanted.

"How soon can I see a quote? And how soon can you start?"

Bill retrieved a business card from his shirt pocket. "I should be able to have the quote to you in twenty-four hours. We can start in about nine or ten days, if that works for you."

"Okay." That meant he would be gone when most of the work was being completed. He should call Adam. Ask him to oversee the project.

"I'll email it to you, yes?"

"Yes, and I'll receive the invoices for the entire remodel."

"Great," he offered his hand to Grandma, then Blake. "I look forward to working with you on this project."

After Blake had let Bill out, he went to his grandma in the kitchen. "Grandma, I won't be able to be here the whole time while they remodel your bathroom."

"Oh, that's alright dear. Adam will be here." She smiled and patted his arm. "I just appreciate you doing all of this for me. You are so generous." She wrapped her arms around him. He reciprocated, and let her love fill his heart. He was a sucker for making his grandma happy.

She released him and lifted her head to meet his gaze. "Now, tell me. How is Charlie?"

Okay, that came from nowhere. "She's good."

"Good? Okay. Are you seeing her tonight?"

"Um, yes," he hesitated, not certain where the questions were leading.

"Good. Then I don't suspect I'll be seeing you until morning." With eyebrows raised, not waiting for a response, she patted him again and stepped away. "I need to go finish my letter and call Gladys."

"Okay, Grandma," and he watched her walk away. He shook his head. His grandma didn't hold back, did she? Feisty woman. The good news—she seemed to have given him permission to stay out the night. All night.

Charlie finished work with enough time to give herself a full-on pampering. Shaven, moisturized, plucked, scented, curled, and topped off with a precise application of makeup, she was ready. *There is no way in hell Blake will be the gentleman tonight!*

She slipped on some satiny unmentionables and tugged her jeans over her hips. Next, she selected a fire engine red sweater with a nice scoop in the front and laid her jacket across the back of the sofa. Ready for her prince, she had time to sip a glass of chardonnay.

When she greeted Blake at the door, she nearly came right there. Dressed from head to toe in black, his sexy body screamed *I'm at your disposal.* His clean-shaven face and smoldering eyes asked, *Aren't you going to touch me?*

"Well hello, handsome."

He didn't conceal his gaze traveling the length of her body. "Hello, yourself. You look good enough to eat."

"Oh, please." *Then let's ditch the movie.* "C'mon in. Want some wine?"

"Thanks. I think I will." He grabbed her hand, spun her around, and pulling her close, he crashed his lips over hers. The pace of the kiss was gentle, though, coaxing her tongue with his. His hand caressed her back as his mouth danced with hers. With her one free hand, she grazed over his shirt feeling the sumptuous ab muscles hiding underneath.

The kiss ended, and she was nearly breathless. And her fresh thong, moist.

"Thank you. That is a delicious wine. Now, shall we go?"

He appeared anxious. Of course, she could just be projecting. "Sure."

She tossed back the last of her wine, and when she turned around, he had moved to the living room. He stared down at her coffee table.

She forgot. She'd left her work out on the table.

She approached him cautiously. This could backfire on her in the worst kind of way.

"What's this?" He pushed her papers and mock-ups around, spreading them out on the table.

"I'm making some marketing collateral for Green Earth Sporting Goods. Print ads, a tri-fold, the usual."

He glanced her way. His eyes, dark and serious.

He refocused on the art. She knew he saw the photos of himself.

"You did this?" Clearly, a rhetorical question.

Was he mad? Her tongue swiped her bottom lip repeatedly. She waited.

He looked, read, moved more papers. God, she should say something.

"I wanted to tell you about the photos. I don't even know if they'll use them, or have me use some of their own instead."

His eyes shot her way briefly, then he transferred his attention back on her work. His silence was killing her.

Finally, he spoke. "This is good." Still looking down, he said, "This is really good."

She let out a shaky breath.

"You're not mad?"

"Mad?" His eyebrows furrowed when he looked at her. "Not at all. These are great." He stood upright. "You are so talented." He closed the space between them and held her hands. "Have always been, and your talent is only growing."

"Thank you," she breathed, barely able to get the words out. Hearing his accolades made her heart sing.

He glanced down at her lips and licked his own. The look in his eyes and the wrinkle in his brow told her he warred over his thoughts.

His voice dropped. "You are amazing, Charlie. You know what I think?"

She swallowed and peered up at him. "What?"

"I think seeing this," he waved a hand toward the coffee table. "Seeing how talented you are, makes me fucking want you."

Her mouth went dry.

His thumbs lightly circled over her wrists. "And I can't. I can't take advantage of you every time we're together."

Her lungs filled with air. "It's only 'taking advantage' if the other party loses something in the deal. Will I lose something, Blake? Or will I gain something?"

His eyes showed a deep blue richness. Clasping her hands behind her back with one hand, the other lifted her chin, aligning her lips with his. He grazed his lips over hers. His hand cradled her cheek as he took the kiss deeper.

Pulling her body flush to his, his growing erection pressed into her deliciously.

"You are fucking amazing." Tugging on her hands, he

backed her one slow step at a time against the wall.

"I'm afraid we're not going to make the movie tonight," he whispered with a glint in his eyes.

His mouth claimed hers. She mewled into his mouth.

She felt his hand slide down her arm and under her sweater to her stomach. Her stomach muscles hitched, and she gasped at his rough fingertips dancing over her skin. Two fingers slid along her waistband leaving a trail of goosebumps on her abdomen.

His actions brought on more wetness to her nether parts, and the ache she'd felt all day was now begging for relief.

She was helpless. Pinned against the wall, her wrists held by his large hand, and his lips locked with hers. He held her where he wanted her, and thank the heavens. She was getting what she'd desired all day.

Her jeans button popped under his skilled fingers. "These jeans hug you like a second skin, Charlie. Did you wear these to turn me on?"

He didn't wait for her answer. "Keep your hands where they are."

He let go of her wrists and instantly tugged her jeans over her hips to the floor. His face mere inches from her sex. He kissed her over her panties causing her to moan. With two fingers looped around her thong, he lowered the fabric to the floor.

"Step out," he commanded.

She did, her legs trembling in anticipation.

"Charlie, I can't wait much longer," was the last thing he had said before his mouth covered her sex and his tongue stroked between her lips. Her hips convulsed.

His tongue worked her to the point she felt her moisture trickle down the inside of her thigh. Her teeth biting her lower lip. She heard his belt buckle come unfastened.

He stood without warning. "Hold on to me."

Then he lifted her, cupping her bare ass. Her legs looped around his waist, and wedged against the wall, he drove into her.

"Ah!" she called out.

"Christ! Did I hurt you?" he paused briefly.

She shook her head, unable to speak.

He began to move again, systematically stroking her deep inside. His size filled her and then some. Her orgasm building from deep inside.

His lips plunged over hers right after he murmured, "Beautiful."

"God, Blake," she gasped. "You feel incredible."

"Charlie, I can't keep my hands off of you. I try and fail miserably."

"I'm so glad . . . you failed. Ah . . . Soon."

He pumped into her several more times when she felt the muscles of her vagina quiver. Her eyes squeezed shut, and her orgasm raced through her body like lightning. She cried out. Blake's orgasm wasn't far behind. His body pressed against hers, against the wall, he breathed into her neck. Both of them gasping for air.

Slowly, she unhooked her ankles. He loosened his grip and lowered her to the floor.

"Let me run to the bathroom and clean up. Help yourself to a napkin."

She smiled the whole way to the bathroom. She could still smell the sex on her. Sex with Blake felt different this time. Amazing. It was better than their college days, and she thought it was pretty rockin' then!

Butterflies did a little dance in her stomach.

The best thing she could do would be to maximize the benefit of having him here while she could. Her heart may not be thrilled with the decision, but what choice did she have? Soon enough, he would leave for Chicago, and she'd be back to party of one.

Chapter Sixteen

So much for being a gentleman, he thought. Charlie did that to him. Gave him uncontrollable urges. Always had. Probably always will.

He wiped and put himself back together. After a few minutes, Charlie came back, half-naked, debauched, disheveled, and sexy as hell. His cock revived quickly.

"Tell me why you're looking at me like I'm a seven-course dinner."

He grinned. "Sorry. I blame you."

"Me?" she asked putting her clothes back on.

"I told you, I can't keep my hands off you," he said low in her ear from behind her. His hands clasping her curvy hips made him want to strip those jeans right off her.

She turned in his arms. "Well, mister. I've worked up an appetite, so it would be best if you fed me," she smirked.

"Agreed. How about I order some Chinese take-out?"

"Great. The menu should be in that top drawer, left of the fridge."

The food arrived several minutes later, and Blake had already opened the wine and poured two glasses. They devoured most everything in front of them. He loved that Charlie had a great appetite.

She glanced down at her watch. "Perfect timing," she announced.

"For what?"

She sprang up and trashed the empty cartons, and replied, "For my favorite show."

Okay, that piqued his interest.

She turned on some cable cop show, grabbed her wine, and called him over. "You'll like it."

He sat for a while trying to get a line on who the characters were. She seemed amused when he asked a question.

"Do you not watch TV in Chicago, Blake?"

He faced her. "Not really. I'm usually on the computer."

"Are you always working on the computer?"

"Mostly, but sometimes I play games."

"I see. Is that it?"

He tilted his head. "Do you mean, am I looking at porn?"

Her head spun his way, her eyes wide. "No! Oh God. No. I meant do you do anything else for de-stressing? What do you do for fun?"

He couldn't help by smile at her reaction. "I do fun things. But now that you bring it up . . . I could take pictures of you, for when I go back." He tended closer and whispered in her ear. "You could be my porn."

Her shiver did not go unnoticed. She liked the idea.

"You're crazy. Now shut up so I can watch."

He reached for her hand and placed it over his rising erection. She looked his way again, her mouth gaped slightly.

"You're recording this show. Let's watch it later. I've got some other ideas right now."

She bit her lower lip but didn't stop him.

He shifted on the sofa, hit the mute button, and reached for his phone. He quickly snapped a picture of her with that sexy red sweater.

"Hey! I wasn't smiling."

She grinned so he snapped some more.

"Now lie back," he told her.

As she scooted, looking a bit apprehensive, he silenced his phone so he could snap as much as he wanted without her feeling self-conscious by the noise.

He propped his arms on the sofa, positioning himself over her. He kissed her gently, and whispered, "Charlie, I won't take any pictures you don't want. And I won't do anything with them. This is between you and me."

They'd taken many pictures of one another before, but none of them had been like what he had planned.

She bit her lip again.

"Do you trust me?"

She nodded and a small smile fell on her lips.

He would work slowly. Not because he wanted pictures, but because he wanted Charlie to savor everything he did to her.

After getting one photo of her lying down, he raised her

sweater to reveal her flat stomach. He kissed her there and dipped his tongue into her navel. Phone in one hand, his thumb hovered over the picture button and snapped shots indiscriminately. He didn't know what he was shooting, but that wasn't his goal. Getting inside of Charlie, making her cry with pleasure, that was his ultimate goal.

The pictures would just be memories. Reminders of this time together when he was home alone in Chicago and wanted to think of her again.

He rested the phone on her stomach and raised her sweater up. "Arms up."

She lifted her hands and rested them on the armrest above her head. With two hands he pushed her sweater up and left it, holding her wrists in place.

He held his phone again and snapped. He closed in on her mouth, not quite kissing her. Her chin lifted as she stretched for the contact. He teased her with the swipe of his tongue. The shutter button depressed. Finally, he covered her mouth with his, claiming her. Her tongue moved with his. He loved hearing her moans.

He slowly pulled away, and she reached her head again for him. He trailed kisses down her neck, her chest, toward her nipples poking against her bra.

Her arms moved.

"Uh-uh."

"Let me touch you."

He smiled and gave her a head shake. "Not yet."

He went back to his task and soon her bra showed wet spots where his mouth had been. He blew, causing her to jerk at the cool sensation.

"Are you wet yet, Charlie?"

He didn't wait for a response. With his free hand, he worked her jeans' button and zipper, capturing his movements on camera. He managed to wiggle her jeans over her hips when she lifted, and he dragged them to her knees.

Her matching bra and panties would show well on the camera.

"Your body is gorgeous, Charlie."

With just his fingertips, he smoothed over her sex. He watched her reaction. Her lips were parted and her dark eyes filled with longing, waiting for him to take it farther.

He slipped a finger under her satin thong to find her incredibly slick. His cock grew to its maximum as he thought about pressing into her warm, wet channel. He dipped a finger in and stroked her slowly. Her back bowed off the sofa. His balls ached now.

"Ready for some more, baby?"

She nodded, perhaps too turned on to speak.

He lifted his finger to her mouth, smoothed her wetness on her bottom lip, then leaned forward to lick it off.

"You taste good."

His anticipation rose, but he needed to keep control. Drawing this out for Charlie's pleasure meant more than a quick lay. No matter how turned on he was.

He slid his hand under her torso and unhooked her bra. Carefully, gauging her reaction, he lifted her bra to rest on her wrists with her sweater.

"Beautiful," he murmured as his fingers stroked over her

full breasts and nipples. He tweaked a nipple with his thumb and forefinger. She gasped and arched her back. That would be an amazing shot.

He laved on her breasts, sucked and toyed with her nipples until they were hard as stones. He had to keep moving, eager to taste her before he slid deep inside.

He stood and grabbed the hem of her jeans and threw them aside. His fingers glossed up one leg to her warm core. Her legs widened. Gently, he played with her thong, slipping a finger under and grazing her hard nub. She felt like a dream. He would have her looking like a dream on his camera too. It would be so good, she would love them.

Gently, slowly, he shifted her panties to the side, revealing her swollen pink lips. He snapped more.

"Blake," he heard her whisper.

"Do you want me to stop?" Had he gone too far?

To his surprise, she shook her head. "I need to come."

The corners of his lips rose. "You will. I promise. Very soon."

He refocused on smoothing the moisture around, caressing her. The whole area glistened. He lowered his mouth, tonguing her clit and slit, delighting in her deep moan.

He paused long enough to say, "I will buy you new panties, Charlie," and reached underneath to the narrowest part and snapped the fabric in two. He moved the strip up, fully revealing her sex. Beautiful.

He kissed and gently sucked her clit pushing from her pump folds. He knew she was close to coming, and he wanted to be right there with her.

Raising his torso upright, he undid his shirt and jeans with one hand. "Legs wider, baby."

She did as he bid.

He slid one finger inside her. Her eyes fluttered shut. Then he pushed in a second finger, and she moaned long and loud.

He took his cock out and slowly drew the tip through her wetness.

She lifted her hips to meet him. He unhurriedly slid into her and almost forgot to capture the joining. He could have sworn he died and gone to heaven.

"Oh God, Blake."

"Tell me, baby."

"You feel so good. So good. It's never been like this," she panted.

"I know, baby."

He pumped into her as he leaned forward to seize her mouth. He snapped anything and everything blind. Her legs hooked high around his waist. He leveraged his arm against the sofa, arched his back and rhythmically pumped deeper and deeper into her her. Charlie's moans grew louder in his mouth. When he felt her muscles pull on his cock, he knew she was coming. He released the kiss and pushed back to capture her face as she came. She was fucking beautiful.

He released his own climax, dropped the phone on the carpet, and rested on her. She flung the sweater and bra off her hands and swung her arms around his neck, breathing heavily.

They lay in their embrace for several moments before she muttered, "Those should be some interesting photographs."

He chuckled into her neck. "Yes. Unfortunately, nothing you can use for marketing."

She laughed, and it was like music to his ears. "You got that right."

Feeling calmer, he rose his head to look at her and asked, "Can I spend the night, Charlie?"

Her eyes twinkled. "Sure, but don't you have to get back to your grandma?"

He shook his head. I think she has her friend looking out for her."

Right then, no better offer could be made. She wanted Blake in her bed. Feel his heat next to her all night. Wake with him by her side in the morning.

They cleaned up, slipped on some t-shirts and sweats, and lounged on the newly christened sofa to finish watching her cop show. She thought back to the amazing sex they had on her sofa. A sofa she would keep forever. Even when the thing got old and tattered, she'd keep it someplace else, in another room.

What they shared, she'd never forget. He wanted only to make her feel good, feel cherished. The connection they had was immensely powerful. So powerful it could cause her to cry if she let it. He was the love of her life. Even as they moved on with their lives, perhaps getting married to other people, her soul would belong to him and his to her.

She sighed and pulled his arm closer across her front. She would miss him when he left—his smell, his touch, the way he'd make her laugh.

Her heart would be ripped to shreds, but she'd never forget—they were one.

Chapter Seventeen

She felt deliciously sore. Sometime during the night, Blake aroused her, made her wet with his fingers and tongue, and slid into her again. He was insatiable. Not that she was complaining.

Actually, come to think of it, she did have a small complaint. He'd entered her from behind and bracketed her arms in a way she couldn't reach back and touch him, fondle and caress him.

He groaned what sounded like "good morning."

She rolled over and propped herself on an elbow. "I have a bone to pick with you."

His eyes opened fully. "You do?"

"Why is it when we're having sex, I can't touch you?"

He smiled. "You can touch me."

"Bullshit."

His lips pursed. "I don't like to admit this, Charlie, but I'm afraid I won't be able to hold out for you if you're touching me."

"Really?" she asked, her voice softer.

"Yes. Like you said last night. It's different this time."

His words set off fizzies in her belly.

She sat up, letting the blanket fall, revealing her naked body to him. "So how long do you think you can last?"

He grinned. "I don't know." His hand moved to touch her.

"Uh-uh. Hands over your head."

His smile could light up a darkened room. "Alright," he said and stretched both arms over his head, leaning them against the headboard.

She made a show of looking at the clock. Then set about torturing him. She kissed his face and neck while her hands roamed his gorgeous body. She pulled the blanket back, uncovering his marvelous cock, long and thick and ready for her mouth.

Her hands smoothed his powerful thighs as her lips kissed his abs and continued south. When she arrived at his darkened head, she licked the slit and teased him.

His growl brought so much delight.

She encased him with her lips and wet him with her tongue. She retracted and gave a gentle blow over his fine equipment.

"Fuck," he bit out.

"Make it last, *baby*." She threw out his pet name for her.

She positioned herself between his legs and stroked his cock with her fingers. She rather liked their role-reversal.

She fisted him completely and covered him with her mouth. He tasted like salty, hot male. She moved her mouth and her fist in tandem, sucking on the way up.

His hips jerked, and he moaned.

"Not yet, *baby*."

She teased and tortured him with little random swipes and licks—his cock, his balls, his thighs. She could see him flex to raise himself closer to her mouth.

She worked extra saliva and lubricated his cock with her mouth. She pulled back, and with the fingertips from both hands, she gently stroked him up and down.

"Fuck, woman." His eyes pinched shut.

She didn't know how much longer he could hold off. Her hands pressing down his thighs, she lowered her mouth and sucked the hell out of him.

He grabbed a pillow, juddered his hips, and cussed up a storm as she worked him energetically.

In no time, he shot his load. At that moment, she pulled back and let him come on her chest. It was warm and wildly erotic. When he was done, she massaged the semen into her chest and breasts as he watched with heavily lidded eyes.

He didn't move, likely drained from his orgasm. "That was the best blowjob I've ever had."

She smiled. She lay down beside him, her head on his chest, and pulled the blanket over them. They could doze a while before they needed to get up.

She drifted off to sleep shortly after him, a smile on her face.

The following ten days were insanely great, to use Charlie's words. They ate, drank, and made love passionately.

When they went hiking the day before, he was so turned on by her, he knew he had to have her. He couldn't wait until they returned home.

He guided her off the path, deeper into the woods. He coaxed her, *Please let me slide inside you. I've been watching those gorgeous legs all day, and I can't wait another moment.*

He'd loosened her shorts to gain access and caressed her. She'd widen her stance, and he knew she was almost ready.

She held onto a tree, face-first, while he eased her shorts down to the ground. He heard a light rustling in the distance. The sound was too light to be another hiker, but what if . . .

He whispered into her ear as he massaged her ass, *What if someone was watching us right now?* He spread her apart with his hands, aligned his cock, and slowly slid into her. *What if there's a man watching me slide into your gorgeous pussy, wishing it was his cock.* She moaned.

He pushed her sweatshirt higher up her back, then reached around to tease her clit. *What if he's watching your beautiful ass and getting hard, wanting to touch you like I am doing now?*

She'd moaned louder and after several seconds, her muscles tightened around him. She lowered her mouth into her arm, covering the moans from her climax. He came at the same time, growling low in her ear.

Most days she would work in her office while he worked at her kitchen table. She would show him her mock-ups over dinner, sometimes asking his advice. One afternoon, they finished work early to look at the photos he'd taken of them having sex on her sofa. They were hot!

And viewing them made him hot again. He took her on the living room rug, the shower, and finally they landed in bed. They didn't even eat dinner that night because they were too exhausted.

The next morning, he'd awoke in a great mood, again, but famished. He cooked enough food to feed an army.

Their time together was so great he dreaded going back to Chicago. Which was hard to admit. He loved what he did—his job, his company, the people. It was like he'd rather be here than there.

But that just wasn't an option.

He stowed some tools in his grandma's tool box when the sound of his cell phone pulled him back to the present.

George.

Shit! His stomach clenched. He had a bad feeling about what George had to share. Did he have to answer it? Life was good. He didn't want to ruin it. The phone rang a second time.

Charlie dropped off the final proofs to Green Earth Sporting Goods. The general manager seemed captivated. His eyes sparkled as she flipped through each piece of marketing collateral.

She waited patiently for his thoughts, chewing on her inside cheek.

"Charlie, I have to tell you, I'm impressed." His opened the tri-fold again and held it open with two hands, nodding slowly. "When my wife told me to give you a chance, instead of the ad firm in town, I thought she was crazy."

"Well, thank you Mister Munoz. Who is your wife?"

"Brenda Munoz," he replied and glanced her way. "I thought you knew."

Brenda Munoz was one of her professors at CSU. Probably the best professor at the university, and that was saying a lot. What a huge compliment that she would recommend her to her husband.

Charlie shook her head and smiled. "No, sir. And I need to be sure to thank her."

"Well, like I said I'm impressed. I like what I see. Maybe we can make a few tweaks, then let's send this to print."

"Okay," she nodded and opened her notebook to jot down his changes.

By the time the meeting was over, Charlie felt like she could fly. *Incredible.*

She wanted to celebrate. She drove to the store and bought some filets, a good bottle of cabernet, and shrimp cocktail. Dinner with Blake that night would be extra special.

Mentally she rifled through her lingerie drawer. She thought she might have some skimpy number she could slip on, too. Her whole body started to hum.

"It's easy to move money around in business. Finding it is the challenge," he heard George say. "Did he mention anything about PR and Reputation Management to you?"

Blake ran a hand over his head. "God, George. I vaguely remember it coming up. I told Patrick to put it on hold. That it wasn't a priority."

"I'm certain he brought it up to gain your approval—"

"Yes, well, evidently he didn't need my approval anyway."

George sighed. "That's true."

Blake felt the heat rise in his face. One hand cracked the knuckles of the other. He never cracked his knuckles. "Are we sure it's him?"

"No one else, other than you, has this kind of access, correct? He has a phony website set up and everything."

"Shit." He let out a breath. "How much, George? How much did he steal?"

He heard an extended inhale. "About forty-three thousand dollars."

"Christ."

"I'm sorry, Blake."

He shook his head. "Thanks," he muttered. "I'm glad you found out—sooner rather than later." He closed his eyes and rubbed a hand over his face. "I will take it from here. Don't let on that anything unusual has been found. I'm out of the state. I'll wrap things up and address it with Patrick."

"Of course."

He disconnected the call. What the hell was going on with Patrick? An employee he trusted. Who was now stealing from him!

He would need to return to Chicago early and take care

of this personally. Shit!

The thought of leaving Charlie dug a gaping, black hole in him. He rested his elbows on the table and hung his head in his hands. Things were going so well between them. And aside from Patrick's embezzling, things were going well with the company.

Chapter Eighteen

Blake disconnected the call with Adam. Just as he had expected—Adam couldn't come to Fort Collins any earlier. His high-profile case with LaKendrick Smith had him snowed under. Adam made it clear, there was "no way in hell" he could get to Grandma's sooner.

He reached out to Ty and Jack; they said keeping an eye on grandma won't be a problem. Between the two of them, they'd have it covered.

"How's it going, Blake? Did you call the airline?" his grandma asked as she entered the kitchen.

He let out a breath. "Yes, I'm on the two-forty tomorrow."

She cupped her hands over his cheeks and kissed his forehead. "I'm gonna miss you."

"Me too, Grandma. Ty and Jack will be around."

"Yes, Jack already called me and told me he and Mya were taking me out to dinner tomorrow night."

"Good."

"Have you told Charlie?"

He shook his head. "No. And I'm dreading it."

"I'll bet." She paused a moment. "You know, you could make this work if you wanted to," she said then kissed his head one more time before leaving the room.

Sure, easier said than done.

Charlie had texted him earlier, said she was cooking dinner at her place. At the time he'd read the text he was smiling. Now, there would be no smile as he ruined their evening.

His arm felt like lead as he pressed the doorbell.

"Hey. You don't have to ring. You can just come— What's wrong?" Her smile fell, and it nearly broke his heart.

He closed the door. "Let's sit."

Her eyes were wide and cautious. She could read him well, or perhaps he had a lousy poker face. "I hired a new accounting firm recently. Well, they did an audit on my books."

"What did they find?"

"Someone is embezzling from me. From the company," he corrected.

"Oh, God."

"Charlie," he reached for her hands, "I have to go back early."

"Yes, of course. When do you have to leave?"

He braced himself. "Tomorrow."

Her body stiffened, and he heard her small gasp. "Tomorrow?" she asked softly.

His heart twisted. "I'm sorry."

"No, I understand. I just didn't think it would be so soon."

"I'm afraid if I don't address it immediately, it will turn into something unmanageable and volatile."

"Of course." She licked her lips. "Well, let's enjoy our last night together, shall we?"

God, how can she stay so positive? He nodded even though he felt about as big as a slug.

Blake's news was the last thing she thought she'd be hearing that night. She knew he would be heading back to Chicago soon, but those few extra days would have been good. It would have been something. She would have had more time to get used to the idea of him leaving.

They ate mostly in silence. The filet tasted like cardboard, and the wine tasted flat.

"I'm sorry I ruined our evening," he said breaking the silence.

She reached to cover his hand with hers. "Don't be. It's not your fault. I was rather getting used to having you around," she shared.

"I was getting used to it too."

"Can you at least spend the night?"

He nodded. "Absolutely."

She gave him the first real smile she felt all night. They mostly finished their dinner and lounged in front of the TV. Before they finished a show, he took her hand and let her back to her bedroom.

He stripped them both naked and made love to her all night. She savored everything he did—all his kisses, all his touches, the way he smelled, and the way he called her name. More than once she found herself close to tears, but she fought them. Tears were wasted energy. He was just as sad. They had several wonderful days together, and tomorrow he'd be gone again.

Life must move on, she told herself.

Watching him walk away was one of the hardest things she ever had to do. Even the first time wasn't this hard. Charlie had anger to protect her heart then.

Blake had thought she cheated, didn't trust her, and left without looking back. He acted like an asshole, and she'd been pissed. Watching him leave led to vague relief.

This time—not so much.

They had kept the goodbyes light and pleasant, trying not to make it as if someone had died. Charlie had held back the tears until he drove away, then she walked back into her house, closed the door, and collapsed to her knees sobbing.

⁓

Blake walked into the office Wednesday morning low in energy but high in determination. The flight back to Chicago gave him time to seethe. He was pissed about having to come back early, and he was pissed about Patrick. How dare he steal from him. After everything he did for the man.

He headed straight for his office and took care of a few security things on his PC before calling Patrick in.

"Hey, Blake! You're back."

"I need to see you in my office."

Patrick arrived with a worried look on his face, as he should.

"Close the door, please." He pushed back from his desk and stood. "Have a seat."

Blake hitched his hip on the edge of the desk and eyed Patrick.

"What's up?"

Like you don't know. "It's come to my attention that someone has been embezzling from the company." Patrick adjusted his position and shifted his eyes.

"We are a small company. The only people with full access to the money are you and me, and I know I didn't take any money. So would you care to share something?"

Patrick stared at the floor for several moments. "Times are hard," he muttered.

Blake's eyebrows rose. "That's your defense?"

Blake knew the truth. It was greed. Patrick had a girlfriend, but no kids, no mortgage, and he was well-compensated. With random drug screenings, he wasn't addicted to drugs.

Blake asked if he had a gambling problem, and Patrick denied it. He had just taken the money with no explanation as to why. Blake was at a loss. He was left with no choice but to fire Patrick.

Blake had planned for a security guard with the office

building to be on stand-by and escort Patrick out, in case things got ugly. Next item on his agenda meant hiring a replacement and mending the damage. Blake hoped it led to nothing too severe. Blake still had hopes of selling the company one day.

He shook his head and returned to his desk. Patrick had created more damage in terms of trust than he had financially.

Her days of late seemed less inspiring, less colorful. Charlie knew it was because Blake had left. A few times she drove by his grandmother's house, for no apparent reason. She felt empty inside and merely drifted through the days looking for anything to satisfy the void.

They spoke most days on the phone and exchanged a few emails. She looked forward to his calls like an anxious teenager. Some calls were long—they'd talk about work, and she'd ask for his opinion. He told her about firing Patrick and looking for his replacement.

Some calls were short. He'd have work to do or a basketball game with his friends. But a pit started to form in Charlie's belly. The calls were getting increasingly shorter. Either Blake was trying not to think of her, or he had someone else to help fill his time.

Tears pricked the backs of her eyes, so she forced herself not to think about it. He always had a reason to drop off, but that didn't stop her feelings of unease.

The days were passing slowly. Blake set up interviews for a new comptroller, and called his financial advisor.

"Roger, I need to move a few thousand dollars into a checking account." Having the money available would make it easier to pay for his grandma's bathroom remodel.

"Yeah, you bet. I'll take care of it. I may execute of few more trades as well."

The man was thorough and smart. Over the years, Blake had come to trust Roger with his money, the proceeds from the sale of his first company. To Roger's credit, he didn't make any moves without conferring with Blake first. "Oh yeah?"

"I want to be cautious with all this discussion about China wanting to trade oil in the yuan. That will lower the value of the US dollar."

"Right."

"So, let me look over your portfolio and make sure everything is as it should be. I'll call you in a day or two."

"Great. Thanks, Roger. I appreciate it."

Demolition of his grandmother's bathroom started the next day. Ty and Jack would keep tabs on the progress. Blake's mind wandered to Charlie. They'd spoken several nights in a row. He looked forward to hearing her voice on the phone. He had a hard time admitting that he missed her. His plan to call her less, so he would think about her less, wasn't panning out the way he hoped. He scratched the side of his head.

The last two weeks or so had been grueling, to say the least. Blake hadn't slept well since his trip. His demeanor was grouchy, he knew it, the office knew it. Damen mentioned something to him the previous night.

"Man, you have enough money. Frickin' move to Colorado. Be with her," he'd said.

"I have a company to run, Damen."

"Screw it. Forget it. Sell it now, not later," he'd offered.

"Are you trying to get rid of me?" Blake joked.

Damen grinned. "This is simple, Blake. Would you be happy to be with her? And would she be happy to be with you? If the answer is yes to both of those questions, then the rest is simple logistics."

And before Blake could retort, Damen threw the basketball at his gut, forcing a gust of air from his lungs. Fire rose in his eyes, and Damen chuckled. "Bring it, big man," he said and took a defensive stance to guard his basket.

"Oh, that's how it's gonna be," Blake countered, and the game continued.

That conversation replayed several times in his mind. Damen may have had a point. He needed to fix this. But moving to Colorado? Was that his solution?

Chapter Nineteen

He stopped the rental car in front of Charlie's house. Well, as close as he could get. He noticed immediately four cars parked in front. *What the hell was going on?* It was two in the afternoon.

He knocked on the front door and a young woman answered. "Oh, great. You can start in the living room. If there aren't enough boxes back there, you can take some of these," she said as she pointed to a pile of collapsed moving boxes. *Moving boxes?*

She spun around and headed for the kitchen. He followed and saw two women wrapping dishes and placing them in cardboard boxes.

"Where's Charlie?"

The woman who answered the door looked up and replied, "Um, last I heard, upstairs in her bedroom."

"Thank you," he managed to get out before heading that direction.

All this meant only one thing—Charlie was moving. Blake had just decided to move back to Fort Collins and she was moving away. He'd been gone only three weeks!

He heard rustling in the closet. He walked closer, and saw Charlie, organizing and folding clothes, placing them into boxes.

"What's going on?"

She jumped and gasped. She spun around.

"Blake! Crap on a stick! You scared me." Her hand flew over her heart, then the most amazing smile flew across her face. Faster than he could blink, she jumped over a box into his arms. "Oh my God. What are you doing here?" Her arms looped around him, and her sweet lips crashed over his.

She smelled like springtime. After an all too brief embrace, he released her. "Wait, my question first. Charlie, are you moving?"

She peered up at him. God, she was beautiful. Her hair captured on the top of her head, rosy cheeks without a stitch of makeup, and bright eyes. She wore dark knit pants with a *#chickswagger* t-shirt. The sight of her made his heart swell. He missed her to his core.

She nodded.

His heart seized. "Why? Where?"

Her pink lips curved. "Chicago."

Did he hear that right? "What?"

She bit her lips, hiding her smile. "I knew you couldn't leave your company, so I decided to go there. I'm putting everything in storage, and I'm selling my house."

"What?" His thoughts whirled.

"Why do you keep asking that? Do you not believe me?" She smirked. "I wanted to surprise you," her voice dipped. She reached and cupped her hands on his cheeks. "I love you. I have to be where you are." She smacked her lips against his again. "God, I missed you," she breathed.

"You were moving to Chicago? Even if it meant leaving your family?"

She nodded. "Even if it meant leaving my family."

His heart grew ten-fold.

"Christ, Charlie." He swung his arms around her, lifted her onto her toes, and kissed her madly. She was willing to give up her life there to come be with him.

Her arms swung around his neck, and she moaned into his mouth. They had kissed for several more moments before she broke the kiss.

"My turn. What are you doing here?"

The smile reflected the insane happiness he felt inside. "I'm moving back to Fort Collins."

Her eyes widened. "So you're moving back here, while I was planning to move up there?" She shook her head in disbelief.

He captured that gorgeous mouth of hers one more time. "That would appear so."

With every touch of her soft body and every kiss of her sweet lips, his cock swelled.

"Incredible. So what about your company?"

"I'll run it from here. But first things first," he said in his deep, sexy voice that made her melt inside. He pulled the hem of her t-shirt up and slid his fingers along her soft skin. "Text someone downstairs and tell them they can all go home."

She grinned. "I can't do that. I need to tell them in person."

Lightning fast, he lifted her shirt up over her head and flung it to the side. She gasped. "Okay, but do you really want to go down there naked?"

"You're crazy!" She dashed by him into her room and grabbed the closest shirt she could find.

He indolently followed, pushing the door closed and pulling off his clothes as he sauntered her way.

She held her hands up as he approached, like that would stop him.

"Cell phone, Charlie." His voice dipped when he grabbed her hips and brought her flush to him, letting her feel his eagerness. "I'm not waiting another minute before I make love to you."

Her insides did a little dance.

"What the hell," she resigned and dropped the shirt from her hand.

"Good girl." He released her so she could reach for her cell phone, sitting in the middle of her queen-sized bed.

His large hands stroked up and down her back and covered her ass.

"I can't concentrate when you do that." Despite her words, she didn't want him to stop. He'd come back to be with her. Her heart felt so full.

He began working her pants over her hips and dragged them to the floor. "Ooh, no panties."

She froze momentarily before she continued texting. Faster now. Then she let the phone lay while he caressed her. Her ache in her sex built. He stroked his hands while kissing, nipping, and licking her ass and thighs. She moaned.

He stood. "I missed you," he breathed at her neck. Then his kisses traveled down her back and across her ass. He had a mission—bring her to ecstasy. His finger skated over her slit. She got wetter and wetter with every move he made. And for the rest of his life, he would always work to make her happy. "We're meant to be together, Charlie."

She moaned again as she pushed against his hand. "Yes, Blake."

"You're mine. Always have been." He slid two fingers into her tight channel and gently stroked.

"Ah! Yes, Blake." Her fingers bunched the sheets.

"Wider, Charlie."

She spread her legs wider, and he leaned down to devour her. His tongue circling her clit and lapping her center.

"Oh, God, Blake."

Her muscles began tightening around him. He quickly pulled out.

"Ah!" she shrieked. "What are you doing?" she asked as she looked back.

"Baby, I want to see you come." Then he rose, flicked off her bra, and commanded, "On your back."

She smiled with hooded, sexy eyes. Naked, and his for the taking.

He stripped out of his briefs and settled between her. "Know something, Charlie? I love you. I've always loved you." He slid into her, savoring every glorious warm, wet inch.

She arched off the bed and her eyes fluttered closed.

"Look at me baby. I realized what I was leaving behind. More than anything I want you. I want a life with you." He pumped slowly.

Her eyes grew misty. "Blake," she breathed, her hands gripping his arms.

"Tell me, Charlie."

"I'm yours."

He thrust into her, and she whimpered. She was close, but he didn't want to rush it. He crushed his mouth to hers. She returned the kiss with as much passion as he gave her. He was a fool to think he could live without her.

"I'm not leaving you ever again. And you're not leaving me."

She panted now. Their rapid breathing and the slap of wet skin the only sound in the room.

"Never, Blake. I'm yours," she sucked in air, "and you're mine."

"That's right, baby. Now come with me," he whispered in her ear.

Her eyes sealed closed, her head bowed back as screamed out his name. He released inside her, letting her milk him, and leaving him boneless. He collapsed over her, having half the mind to keep an elbow locked to protect her from his crushing weight. He panted into her neck.

"Oh, how I've missed you." Her hand stroked the side of his face.

He lifted his head to meet her eyes. "I'm here now."

The smile that spread across her face was breathtaking. "And you're staying."

"And I'm *definitely* staying."

The end.

Thank you for reading my story.
I hope you enjoyed it.

Before you go…

Please post a review where you bought it.

Mia would love for you to check out the other Hard Men of the Rockies titles by Chick Swagger authors. Here's a sneak peek at Adam's story…

Blackmail and Lace

A Hard Men of the Rockies novella
by Tracy Ward

I recognized the collection of bumper stickers as I slowly passed. It was Madi's Jeep alright, parallel parked in front of a brand new bar I'd never seen. Her headlights were dim in the way that signaled her battery was running dangerously low.

Shouldn't have surprised me.

She'd always been careless like that. With the winter storm moving in, it would take AAA hours to reach her for a jump. And she could forget about a tow truck. I'd told her for years to either buy a newer model car with automatic lights or stop being so scatterbrained. Now that her commercial decorating business was doing so well, it wasn't like she couldn't afford the newer car option.

The side streets of Fort Collins, Colorado near the Colorado State campus were empty, even for a Monday night in October. But that's what happened with high wind gusts, low wind chill and a deluge of snow just now threatening to fall. Needing to make sure she was okay, I double parked beside her. Finding she'd at least remembered to lock her doors, I hunkered down against the bone-freezing cold and went inside.

Her ass was the first thing I noticed when I walked into the bar.

The second thing was that there were absolutely no customers in the place. Were they even open? I couldn't recall seeing a sign.

A slow grin spread across my face even as a pang of nostalgia tore through my gut like a ripcord pulled on a parachute. We'd really been something together once, back during our carefree high school days. Now we were good friends with occasional benefits. Benefits I hoped to take advantage of at some point during my Colorado stay.

Madi shifted her hips as she bent over an empty table, doing what exactly, I couldn't tell. Her hair was blonder than when I'd last seen her. And longer. But that was to be expected with women. Extensions were becoming the norm, even among the unpretentious like Madi.

It had been months since I'd last seen the woman who'd once been my fiancé, if you could call our spontaneous and short-lived idea of commitment when we were eighteen an engagement. Months since my Grandma Rosie's heart attack had me and the rest of my family running back to Fort Collins to be by her side, afraid for the worst. But it had only been days since the end of the LaKendrick Smith trial, where *Adam Holder* had become a household name. And I was still riding high and feeling invincible, coming off the greatest victory so far in my legal career.

I probably should've given Madi a heads up that I was coming back to town, but that just wasn't our way. Since I'd be around for the next four weeks, helping my cousins update and remodel Grandma Rosie's family home, my plan had been to look her up later. Even if Madi hadn't been my first priority, she wouldn't begrudge me from admiring the view before I made my presence known.

She shifted again, causing her flannel shirt to ride up. A mismatched, purple lace camisole peeked out from underneath. She wore black boots with a thick, minky-fur lining. They came up just above her calf and were sturdy yet stylish if there was such a thing for snow boots. Her leggings, made of high quality dri-fit material, stretched taut across her backside in a way that conjured caveman fantasies, ensuring the survival of the species for billions of years to come.

I'd gotten so used to seeing women covered in business suits after showering in feminism that I'd forgotten what this—the watching of a salt-of-the-earth woman doing an unspecified task—could do to a man. In D.C., where I now lived, women were powerful, sexy, and smart as hell. But nothing could compare to the draw of a strong, equally smart and beautiful, home-grown Colorado girl.

The frigid breath of wind rattled the windows, but even that sound didn't faze her.

Soon she straightened.

I saw a clipboard and pen in her hand, the colored-cord of earbuds hanging from her ears.

Without thinking of consequences, my palm wrapped

around her hip and gave it a squeeze.

She reacted quickly, bringing her elbow up and around.

Years of football training, dodging hits and tackles, kicked in and I ducked, circling her around to face me as I did. Trying to keep us both on balance, I gripped the bottom of her flannel shirt. The material gave when she swung from the opposite direction.

The *rrrriiiippppp* and *thwack* happened at the same time. Buttons scattered just as an explosion went off in my temple.

From the center of her chest, she yanked the earbud cord from her ears.

"Whoa, angel. I didn't mean to…" I watched as she pushed her hair out of her face. My stomach dropped. "Shit. You're not Madi."

About the Author

Mia London loves to write.

After reading fiction for years, she decided it was finally time to put those images and scenes floating around in her head down on paper.

She is a huge fan of romance, highly optimistic, and wildly faithful to the HEA (happily ever after). Her goal is to create a fantasy you will enjoy with characters you could love.

She lives in Texas with her attentive, loving, super-model husband, and perfectly behaved, brilliant children. Her produce never wilts, there are no weeds in her flowerbeds, and chocolate is her favorite food group.

Then she wakes up.

Facebook:

http://on.fb.me/1mY5RSr

Twitter:

@MiaLondonAuthor

Goodreads:

www.goodreads.com/author/show/8414916.Mia_London

Amazon:

www.amazon.com/Mia-London/e/B00MI216L0/

Webpage:

http://www.mialondon.com/

Email:

mia@mialondon.com